Breathless Descent

TEXAS HOTZONE SERIES BOOK THREE

NEW YORK TIMES BESTSELLING AUTHOR

LISA RENEE JONES

ISBN-13: 979-8704345978

www.lisareneejones.com

BE THE FIRST TO KNOW!

The best way to be informed of all upcoming books, sales, giveaways, televisions news (there's some coming soon!), and to get a FREE EBOOK, be sure you're signed up for my newsletter list!

SIGN-UP HERE:
http://lisareneejones.com/newsletter-sign-up/

Another surefire way to be in the know is to follow me on BookBub:

FOLLOW ME HERE:
http://bookbub.com/authors/lisa-renee-jones

PROLOGUE

CALEB MARTIN LEANED against the Fresco Club bar, watching as Shay White celebrated being old enough as of today to dance the night away at the over-eighteen hot spot. Trying his best not to notice the way her red, silky dress accented her tiny waist and each sultry move of her slender but curvy hips. Oh, yeah, he thought, watching her dance with some guy from her school, it hugged those hips and her heart-shaped backside in a far too seductive way. And when said "boy" slid his hand to her waist and sidled up close to her, Caleb tightened his hand on the beer he held until he thought he heard glass crack.

"Should I go take care of that, or do you want to?" asked Kent White, Shay's big brother and Caleb's best friend since grade school. The fast pop tune changed to a slow, sultry tune, and the boy's hand slipped to Shay's backside.

Kent set his beer down so hard it splattered. "Oh, hell, no." He charged toward the dance floor, and silently, Caleb cheered him onward, watching as Shay flipped her long blond hair over her shoulder and shoved her hands onto her hips to square off with Kent.

Caleb had wanted that hand off Shay's butt and now it was, thankfully—and if he was honest with himself, it wasn't brotherly protectiveness fueling that desire when it should have been. After all, the Whites had taken Caleb in six years before, and treated him like family after he'd lost both his parents in close progression at the ripe young age of fifteen. He felt like family, too. Heck, in a family filled with fair hair and eyes, he even *looked* like family with his sandy brown hair and light green eyes.

But for the past two years, since about the time Shay had turned sixteen, she'd been flirting with him. Even back then, he'd been smart enough to know nineteen was too old for a sixteen-year-old, regardless of the fact that she was like a sister to him. And so, Caleb had quickly, and frequently, discouraged her advances.

Tonight though, her teasing looks and purposeful smiles, when combined with that dress—that sexy-as-hell dress—had the man in him standing at attention. Had him wondering what she would taste like, what she would feel like in his arms.

As if she sensed what Caleb was thinking, her gaze whipped to him, and he felt that gaze like a punch right in the groin. Oh, yeah, he would have been a fool to believe he was going to resist Shay when she joined him at the University of Texas next month, and one thing Caleb Martin was not—was a fool. Thus why he'd made a long-debated decision official. He was leaving in a week. And not to head back to campus. She just didn't know it yet. She was the only one who *didn't know*. He'd sworn the family to secrecy until after she'd celebrated her birthday. He'd just found out his enlistment orders and he didn't want anything to ruin her party, or the bond he had with her or the family. And the temptation that was Shay White was a one-way ticket in that direction and he knew it. He had to say goodbye.

Emotion welled in his chest, and he tore his gaze from hers. With a scrub of his face, Caleb sat his beer down and headed to the bathroom. Tomorrow he became a soldier, exactly like his pops, who'd died a hero saving another soldier's life. It was the right decision for Caleb, one that had called to him for a good while, and he was finally answering.

It was several minutes later, when he exited the bathroom into the tiny hall, his cowboy boots scraping the wooden floor, that he found Shay waiting for him.

"The Army?" Shay demanded, waiting for him in the narrow hallway. "When were you going to tell me?"

"Thanks, Kent," he mumbled under his breath. "I was going to tell you, Shay. Just not on your birthday, and Kent knew that."

"Don't," she said, and flung herself into his arms, all soft and warm and emotional. "Don't leave." Her chin tilted upward, her eyes filled with tears. "I can't bear the idea of something happening to you."

More of that damnable emotion welled in his chest. "Nothing is going to happen to me," he promised.

"Like nothing happened to your father?" she said. "No. I won't let you go. I..." She pushed to her toes and pressed her lips to his.

Caleb froze for an instant, but then that emotion, that deep burn he'd had for her, rose to the surface. She was right. His father had died in war. Hell, his mother had died of a heart attack. He could die, too. Once he left, he might well never come back, and he wasn't going to die with any regrets. And never kissing her would be a regret.

He slid his hands into her hair, slanted his mouth over hers and kissed her—deeply, sensually, hungrily, reveling in the innocent sweep of her tongue against his. He moaned with the taste of her. Then reveled in the echoed, soft moan that escaped her lips, in the sway of her body into his.

Laughter permeated the passion threatening him, then voices. Caleb quickly ended the kiss and settled her away from him. Guilt twisted in his gut. “I’m sorry. That shouldn’t have happened. It was a mistake.”

“I’m not,” she whispered. “I’m not sorry.”

Kent rounded the corner, ending any further conversation, wiping away the moment, but not the kiss. The kiss had not only happened, it had changed everything for Caleb and Shay. A kiss worthy of sending a man off to the Army, maybe to war, and a kiss to justify why leaving was the right decision.

1

"IS HE COMING?"

"Is who coming?"

Shay set down the knife that she was using to touch up the icing on her parents' fortieth anniversary cake and glared at her older brother, Kent. "You know who."

"Caleb," he said, and reached for a strawberry from the bowl next to the cake.

Shay smacked his hand. "Don't eat the food before the guests arrive, and who else would I be talking about? Of course—*Caleb*." Just his name twisted her in knots.

"So is he?"

Kent snatched a strawberry and bit down. "Yes, he's going to be here. Why wouldn't he be? It's Mom and Dad's anniversary. They're his parents, too."

"He's been home for a few months," Shay said, "and I've yet to see him. That's why." And because she'd kissed him. Ten years ago, on her eighteenth birthday, and they'd hardly seen each other since. "He came home all of a handful of times in a decade."

Kent snorted. "What did you expect? He was in the Special Forces. Some elite unit that he can't even talk about. And *you* might not have seen him since he's been home, but I have."

"Because you went to that skydiving business of his and jumped out of a plane." A sales rep for a high-end sporting goods company, her brother didn't get his sun-kissed, athletic good looks by accident. He was all about sports, the more extreme, the better. "You went to him, Kent. He didn't come to you."

"He's trying to get his business rolling," he said. "Cut him some slack. There's nothing more to this. Don't read into it. Ever since you opened that fancy psychology practice of yours, you're always reading too much into things."

"I just don't want Mom and Dad to be disappointed," she said. "Today is special."

"He'll be here," her brother reassured her. The doorbell rang. "That must be the caterers." He glanced at his watch. "And not a minute too soon. We don't need thirty hungry people roaming around our backyard. It might get dangerous." He started to turn away and seemed to think twice. He leaned on the counter. "Stop fretting. He'll be here. And Mom and Dad will have a great day."

She forced an accepting nod she didn't feel. Kent continued to study her with a keen look until the doorbell rang again. Then, with a scrub of his jaw, he departed. She knew he could tell something more was going on with her than simple worry over her parents' party—she'd seen it in his eyes—and there would be questions later she didn't intend to answer.

Shay shoved her long blond hair behind her ears and crossed her arms in front of the modest swimsuit cover-up. Her mother had volunteered her to put her college lifeguard skills to work today with the many kids attending the party. Caleb had been a lifeguard, too, she thought, unable to escape memories of his role in her past. She squeezed her eyes shut at the vivid image of him in red lifeguard trunks, bare-chested, with a sprinkling of hair over perfectly defined pecs. His light brown hair streaked with blond from the sun.

Green eyes glistening with amber flecks. And the lifeguard whistle. The man made that whistle so darn sexy, as silly as it might seem. How many times had she silently vowed to one day blow that whistle?

She shook herself, appalled at how ridiculously capable of recalling his "whistle" she was, despite a full decade since he'd donned said red trunks. Or how easily she remembered the moment she'd pressed her lips to his, how firm and smooth and wonderful they'd been. And the way he'd let out a soft moan that had told her he'd hungered for the kiss as much as she had, even if he'd never have claimed it himself. It had been her turn to moan when his hand had slid to her back and molded her close.

And then, true to form, Kent had shown up. Caleb had bolted so fast you would have thought he'd been struck by lightning. He'd told her the kiss had been a mistake and left.

The next week, after an awkward family farewell, at least for the two of them, he'd been gone. The few times Caleb had made it home in those ten years, the tension between them, the attraction, had been uncomfortably evident. And now that he was home to stay, he was avoiding her. That meant avoiding her family, *their* family.

She straightened, realizing what she had to do. She couldn't let this continue. My God, she was a therapist. She helped people deal with the fastballs of life and reveled in being good at it. She had to deal with her own issues. She and Caleb had to talk, to get whatever was between them out in the open, instead of hiding from it. The damage was done.

She reached for the knife to finish the icing and then pressed her hands to her parents' green marble counter. Who was she kidding? Talking wasn't going to solve anything. Talking wasn't going to dissolve the combustible sexual tension between them. It seemed to Shay there was only one answer. Something drastic. Another kiss. Something she would never have considered if the circumstances hadn't become so strained. Okay, the fantasy about the red trunks helped. But they both needed to know once and for all what was between them. Her plan: she was going to kiss Caleb again, and it was quite possible she wouldn't even enjoy the kiss. Wouldn't that be a relief?

***

THE HOTTEST WOMAN he'd ever seen in his life was poised on the diving board, in a red-and-white, polka-dot bikini. She was also his best friend's twenty-eight-year-old "baby" sister. And considering said best friend was standing next to him, Caleb Martin tried not to drool. It wasn't easy. Shay White had been winding him into a tight ball of lusty need for as long as he could remember.

In fact, if not for the way Shay had rattled his cage, and the secret—albeit ancient—history the two of them shared, Caleb might not have followed in his father's footsteps and joined the Army. Shay had been the ink on the dotted line, the final nudge.

Caleb watched as she bounced on the board, as if intentionally drawing him under a spell where nothing else mattered. There was only the moment, and her on the diving board and in a bikini that, while certainly appropriate for her parents' backyard anniversary party, showed enough skin to entice his imagination to fill in the blanks.

Another graceful bounce and her long, lithe body curved into a delicate arch. Caleb's hungry eyes followed every last glimpse of skin, from fingertips to her shoulder-length blond hair, down to those gorgeous, fantasy-inspiring legs and all the way to her toes, as she slipped into the blue depths of her parents' pool. His heart thundered in his chest. Shay damn near made the water boil. She damn sure made his blood boil. The woman was hotter than the late-July, Austin, Texas, sun beaming through clusters of smoky clouds.

"Always liked to be the center of attention, didn't she?"

Caleb blinked, bringing Shay's brother, Kent, back into focus, along with the twenty-five or so guests mingling in various poolside areas.

"Yes," Caleb agreed, turning the iced bottle of beer cooling his hand to his lips and savoring the much-needed chill as liquid slid down his throat. "Shay was always the center of attention." And Kent had no idea how true that statement really was for him.

"Caleb!" The warm, friendly voice of Sharon White spun Caleb on his heels and into her hug.

"Happy anniversary, Sharon," he said. "Forty is something to be proud of."

"Thank you, son," she said, still hugging him, holding on to him, before leaning back to give him a thorough inspection. "And now that we've both retired from our teaching jobs, we plan to enjoy ourselves a bit."

"You deserve it," he said, thinking of how dedicated they both had been to their high school students. He'd been fifteen, Kent's best friend, and one of Sharon's students, when his mother—who'd been struggling to raise him alone—had died of a heart attack. Years before, Caleb's father had been lost in a military operation overseas.

A familiar scent brought back memories of those years, of when Sharon had become his second mom.

"Do you smell like sugar cookies?" he asked. "Or am I having flashbacks of you baking on the weekends?"

"You were always begging me to bake sugar cookies," Sharon said, smiling. "Which is exactly why I baked a batch and hid them in the pantry for you. I have to do something to get you to come around to see me." She pursed her lips at him, her sleek silver hair coiled at her neck. "You've been out of the Army two full months, and I've seen you two times if you count today. Shame on you, Caleb Martin. That's once a month."

Caleb hung his head, shamed indeed. "I'm sorry," he said, regretting that his fear of running into Shay had made him avoid both Sharon and her husband, Bob. Sharon, in particular. The woman had been his rock—seen him through some secret tears and a struggle for identity. He added, "You *absolutely* will see me more often."

The delicate lines around Sharon's too-keen light blue eyes crinkled in scrutiny. In a motherly gesture, she stretched her arm and touched his light brown hair, then his jaw, her brows dipping. "You look tired." She let out a breath, and concern kicked into a parental lecture. "You and those friends of yours are working too much. I know you want to get that skydiving business of yours off the ground, but you can't go jumping out of planes with no rest."

Caleb figured she didn't want to hear that as recently as two months earlier, sleep had been a luxury, and skydiving into the bowels of hell in some dangerous country was the norm. Instead he promised, "I'm careful. But I have to work hard and get the Hotzone making a profit if I plan to stay a civilian." And he did plan to stay a civilian, a vow—silent or not—he would never have thought possible a year before.

"Plan to stay a civilian," came a soft, silky voice from behind him.

Shay.

"Well," she continued, "you haven't bothered to come see me since you got back into town—*two months ago*."

Tension rippled through Caleb's body in tidal-wave proportions, pulling him under with such force he would have sworn he was drowning in those brief seconds before he turned.

Caleb brought her into focus. Shay—gorgeous, petite, feisty little Shay, with one towel wrapped around her slender figure, tucked under her arms. With a smaller towel, she dried her light blond hair spun with the color of snow-streaked wheat that accented equally light blue eyes brimming with mischief and challenge.

"Now, Shay," Sharon scolded, "don't be giving Caleb a hard time." Sharon chuckled and elbowed Caleb. "Better yet. Please. Feel free. Does my heart good to see you three kids together, stirring up harmless trouble."

Kids? Kent and Caleb were thirty-one. Shay was a mere three years younger. Hardly kids. And any jest between Shay and him was hardly harmless.

"Both you women need to behave." The playful reprimand came compliments of Bob White as he joined them, proudly sporting khaki shorts and a T-shirt that read Forty is the New Thirty. With his blond hair now silvery gray, he remained tall and athletic—an older, wiser version of his son.

"Cut Caleb some slack," Bob ordered. "He's been getting a business started." He kissed Sharon's cheek and then raised a hand to Caleb. "Come 'ere, boy! Give the ol' man a hug."

Another bear hug ensued—in a manly kind of way, of course—before Shay asked, "Where's my hug?"

Caleb's gut clenched, thinking of how she felt in his arms...as she had the night of her eighteenth birthday. The night everything had changed. The night he'd forgotten himself and kissed her. And if not for an interruption, he might have done a whole lot more. No. No "might." He would have. His attraction to Shay was that strong, an attraction that only seemed to age like fine wine—get richer and more irresistible. It was a hard lesson he'd learned on the few visits home that he'd dared while enlisted.

She was in front of him now, driving him insane with her nearness. "Unless you're afraid I'll get you wet?" she taunted softly, her gaze sliding over his jeans and T-shirt, a contrast to everyone else's swim trunks, shorts and various summer attire. "You aren't exactly dressed for the pool." She leveled him with a stare. "You do know the meaning of *pool* party?"

He wanted nothing more than to dive into that pool with Shay, with nothing but swimsuits between them. Exactly why he'd dressed to avoid temptation.

Bracing himself for the impact, he decided to take charge of this unavoidable hug and then make a run for the other side of the pool. Caleb attempted a short, one-armed hug, his beer a great excuse to avoid anything more intimate. "How've you been, Shay?" he asked.

Instantly, her arms wrapped around his neck, preventing his escape. She clung to him, her soft, warm curves melting into him—a friendly embrace to anyone watching, but they both knew it was more. And damn it, it wasn't enough. He'd longed to hold her again for so very long. He wanted to mold her closer, to inhale her, to absorb her.

Among all the women a decade of traveling the world delivered to a Special Ops soldier like himself, none of the fast exits had left him with regret. But leaving Shay had, and often he had wondered if she were the reason why no one else had mattered. Because there was no question—she had long ago reached inside him and refused to let go.

"I missed you, Caleb," she said softly, near his ear.

I missed you, too, he thought, fearing the words would sound as those spoken by a man, not a brother. And he was her brother. Brothers were forever. The minute they became more, they were like every other couple—they could crash and burn, lose what they had. And he'd lose more than her. He'd lose the only family he'd known for the past fifteen years.

He snatched the wet towel she'd draped over his shoulder and tugged it out of her grip, stepped backward and handed it to her. "Thanks for the soggy shoulder, Shay-Shay," he teased, reminding her of their youthful play and putting their relationship where it was meant to be—laden with sibling jest.

"Oh, God," she said, rolling her eyes and wringing the towel in her hands. "Don't call me that. You know I hate it."

Kent chuckled. "You loved it when you were thirteen."

"Thirteen," she repeated, grinding the age through her teeth. "When I played dress-up in Mom's work clothes."

"And transformed yourself into 'Shay-Shay Va-voom,'" Kent added, needling her.

"I hate you, Kent," she said, her teeth still clenched. "Really, really hate you."

Kent snorted his approval. "To a brother, that's the ultimate vow of love. Right, Caleb?"

"Right," Caleb agreed. This was going exactly where Caleb had planned. He tipped his beer, but before the bottle made it to his mouth, Shay snatched it, their fingers brushing, electricity darting between them.

"I'm the youngest," she said, turning up the bottle. "I get what I want." The comment, while innocent enough to everyone else, wasn't innocent at all.

Caleb took back his beer, the intimacy of sharing with her setting him on edge. "Funny thing about this beer," he said. "I got it from the kitchen on the way out here. Every time I go into that kitchen, I think about a certain pair of jeans you used to love."

Shock slid over her face. "Don't even go there, Caleb," she warned fiercely.

Kent snorted. "Oh, yeah. Those *damn* jeans."

"Don't you go there either, Kent," Shay warned. "Or I won't set you up on that blind date with Anna you've been begging for."

Bob chuckled. "Then I guess I'll have to go there for all of us. Why in the world, my little Shay, did you put the jeans in the oven in the first place? Just make me understand. I've always wanted to understand."

"I've answered this question a million times," she said, her pretty, naturally pink lips pursed in frustration. "I was sixteen when I did that. Sixteen! I'm twenty-eight years old and, I might add, a licensed psychologist who counsels people about the trauma of bad memories. In case you didn't know, Daddy, this is a bad memory."

"The dryer was broken," Caleb answered, when unnecessary guilt flashed on Bob's face. No matter how upset Shay acted, she ate up the teasing. And he loved watching her cheeks flush, her eyes light up. "She needed her best jeans for a party." He'd liked those jeans. Liked them too much, considering she'd been sixteen and he'd been nineteen, about to move into campus housing at the University of Texas. Too old for her. Not that he'd ever be the right age for her. But at the time, he'd been damn glad she wasn't prancing around in those damn tight jeans anymore, inviting hound-dog teen boys to salivate.

Shay shot him a scorching look that wiped the smile from his face. He was pretty sure she would have smacked him otherwise.

Sharon sighed. "Men just don't understand how important the perfect jeans are to a female," she said, defending her daughter. "It really was a smart idea, using the oven. It was like a sauna drying room. I think it showed initiative and innovation."

Exasperated, Bob's eyes went wide. "Since when is burning down the kitchen called innovation?"

"How many experiments do you think Thomas Edison tried that went wrong?" Sharon countered protectively.

"What was she trying to create?" Bob replied. "The fastest way to destroy her parents' house?"

"Maybe if you would have put them on warm, not broil, Shay-Shay," Kent offered, sipping a beer. "Your va-voom might not have gone ka-boom." He eyed Caleb. "What do you think, Caleb?"

"I didn't put them on broil!" Shay spat, before Caleb could reply, as she shoved her hands on her hips. The towel fell to her waist, and Caleb gulped at the sight of her high, ample breasts, covered by nothing but thin slices of cloth. "I left them on warm when I went to shower. How was I to know they'd go up in flames?" She clutched the towel and waved a hand between Kent and Caleb. "And how is it that every time you two get together, I'm reduced from grown adult to defensive teenager?"

Kent grinned. "It's a gift."

She huffed. "I've got a gift for you, Kent," she said. "And her name isn't Anna." Her gaze cut back to Caleb. "I know what you just did, and it won't work. Two can play your game, Caleb Martin. You remember that."

She turned on her heel, strutted back to the pool and then let go of the towel. It slid to the pavement, her pert, heart-shaped backside displayed for Caleb's admiration. Caleb silently groaned. The only game he was going to play was the one called "cold shower." Correction, by the time this party was over, the game would be called "*long* cold shower."

2

CALEB HAD BEEN AWAY a long time, but the game of horseshoes as a family had endured. Caleb tipped back a beer as he watched Kent make a toss. There were a good seven or eight guys standing around playing. All family and friends. Some Caleb knew. Some...well, he'd been away a long time.

Bob let out a loud bark of laughter as Kent's shot landed about as close to the target as Caleb was to pretending he didn't know every move Shay made today. Until a few minutes ago, she'd been in the pool, supervising the kids and entertaining them. Sweet, adorable Shay, always generous with her time helping others.

He hadn't been surprised on a visit home years before to discover Shay had started volunteering at her college counseling center, or that the work at the center had led to her changing her major from business to psychology. She'd always had a thing for taking in every stray animal in her path. Kind of like her family had been with him. They had done everything in their power to make him feel he was whole again after losing his parents, as if he belonged. The Army had given him a sense of belonging, but not a sense of family...the way the Whites had.

"Were you aiming for the driveway out front or what, Kent?" Bob asked, and Kent buried his face in his hands, cursing at his truly horrific shot. Kent never handled his beer well. And having been away, Caleb had missed just how true, and entertaining, that fact was. He'd missed a lot of things he'd pretended he didn't miss, that he thought he could do without.

Bob's comment snapped Caleb back to the moment.

Kent glowered and held his hands to his sides in challenge. "You gonna rag on me, too?"

"Nah, man," Caleb said innocently. "I think you know how bad that shot was without me pointing it out."

Rick Jensen, Kent's buddy who'd joined them for the day, added, "You do give new meaning to the saying 'Just Do It.'" As doctor for the University of Texas baseball team, Rick apparently subscribed to Kent's habit of Nike phrase dropping.

"Don't even go there, Rickster," Kent said, grabbing his beer from the ground where he'd left it. "We both know you don't know the meaning of 'Just Do It,' or you would have at least asked Shay out by now. We'd all like her to find a nice guy like you to take care of her, rather than some hound dog."

Caleb wasn't sure whose jaw dropped closest to the ground—Rick's, Bob's or his own. It was a pretty close race. "Damn it, Kent," Rick muttered, looking pale despite his tanned skin and blond hair. "Why can't you ever keep your mouth shut?"

"Shutting his mouth isn't something he excels at," Bob said dryly. "They didn't even have to smack that boy's ass when he was born to get him squealing."

Shay and her love life shouldn't matter to Caleb, so why was every nerve he owned standing on end? Hell, he could almost feel the hair on his arms lifting, his skin tingling.

"You keep waiting for a sign," Kent continued to Rick, as if his father's explanation were a license to continue. "There won't be a sign. Shay's a traditional kind of woman. She doesn't flirt. She doesn't come to you. You go to her. You have to get over these nerves."

Rick didn't look convinced, as he opened his mouth and then shut it.

Bob studied him and asked, "What seems to be bothering you, son?"

His question stiffened Caleb's spine. Bob liked this guy Rick. Hell, Caleb liked Rick. No. Caleb hated Rick.

"She's friendly," Rick said after another moment of hesitation. "But not overly so. I don't want everyone to feel uncomfortable if I'm around after she's turned me down." He laughed. "Or have Kent beat up my ass because I make her mad or something."

There it was. Everything Caleb felt. Everything. So completely, so near exactness, that Caleb about fell over. And Rick didn't call these people family. He had his own. The validation twisted inside him.

"For the record," Kent said, "my sister's a lady, but she don't take no junk. *She'll* beat your ass if you screw up. She doesn't need me to do it. But you have to actually ask her out to ever get the chance for anyone to beat your ass."

"And I so want that opportunity," Rick quipped back sardonically. "You aren't helping."

A sound of frustration slid from Kent's lips, and he motioned to Caleb for help. "Tell 'em, Caleb. Tell Rick if he wants Shay, he has to go after her." He motioned toward the tables of food set up on the opposite side of the yard where Shay stood.

Thankfully, she'd covered her swimsuit with a crocheted shirt of some sort that touched her knees, which at least allowed Caleb to look at her without getting an instant hard-on. Man, he was pathetic.

"Do it. Now. Today. Ask her out," Kent insisted.

Suddenly, Kent's words from moments before radiated through Caleb, like a light being slowly turned from dim to bright. *She doesn't come to you.* Shay didn't approach men. Kent was right. But she *had* approached him. In the past. And even today, she'd openly flirted, hugged him, held on to him, molding those sweet curves against his body, intentionally teasing him. Maybe that meant she really wanted him. Or maybe it meant she had an evil side he didn't recognize—that she enjoyed taunting him, knowing he'd never dare act on his desire. Believing her capable of such a thing would make it easy to walk away, easy to turn away. But deep down, he knew there was no evil to Shay. He knew they shared a bond, a friendship and attraction.

"...like the present. Right, Caleb?"

"Right what?"

"There's no time like the present," Kent repeated and made a fist. "Just do it, Rick."

Caleb inhaled a discreet breath and lifted his beer. "No time like the present. If you are going to do it, do it." Right here, right now, where Caleb could kick Rick's Doctor-Do-Gooder, nice-guy ass if he stepped out of line. Which he wouldn't. He was, after all, a nice guy, but Caleb could hope.

A flickering memory played in his mind. Of Shay pushing to her toes and pressing those soft lips to his. Of her tentative, inexperienced little tongue caressing his. He all but moaned.

"You heard the man," Kent said, waving at Rick. "Just do it, man."

Rick drew a breath and handed Caleb his beer. "Save that for me. I might be needing it."

Rick could kiss Caleb's ass if he thought he was getting his beer back. He wasn't giving Rick anything.

Well, nothing but the woman he wanted and couldn't have. No. Rick was not getting his beer.

***

SHAY STOOD AT the food tables snacking on a plate of cucumbers and ranch dressing, a comfort food since she was a small child. She didn't dare look over at the horseshoe area again. She'd seen enough there to know she didn't need to see any more. Her plan to kiss Caleb again was hereby over. Watching him interact with Kent and her father, along with the rest of their family and friends, had been a reality check. Every second he was here, Caleb relaxed more, fell into the old traditions and inside jokes.

He belonged here, yet he'd stayed away. And she knew why. Because of her. Because she'd kissed him and made him feel uncomfortable. Because he didn't believe they could share an attraction and a family. Which meant her plan to kiss him again, while tempting and all too appealing, was selfish. Wrong.

"Hi, Shay."

Shay jumped and somehow managed to turn the paper plate over and onto Rick's shirt. In the process, one of the cucumber slices flew in the air and landed on his head. She'd just turned one of Kent's work friends into a kitchen sink.

"Oh, my God! Rick. I'm so sorry!" Cringing, she grabbed the cucumber from his head and flung it away, then tossed the paper plate into a trash can. Ranch dip clung to his shirt. "I can't believe I just did that. I was thinking about... I...I'm sorry." Shay grabbed several napkins and offered them to him.

"It's okay," he said, smiling as he wiped the mess on the front of him. "Though it kind of blows the cool-guy image I was going for."

She laughed and said, "You can always judge a guy's coolness by how he handles a plate of cucumbers and ranch dip spilled on his shirt. And considering you don't seem mad at me, you passed with absolute coolness."

He drew a breath. "Then I'm hoping this is a cool enough moment to ask you out to dinner and a movie."

"A...a...?" Yowza, she had not seen that coming. She'd never really had a conversation with him. "Dinner and a movie? I...I don't know what to say."

"How about yes?" he asked hopefully, looking remarkably awkward for a guy who seemed to have plenty of reasons to be confident. He was a good-looking guy, with dark hair and dark eyes and a shy smile. He was a doctor, for a professional sports team to boot. They'd have stuff to talk about. Stuff. Patients. The physical manifestations of stress.

So why didn't she just say yes? Caleb. Caleb was why. Caleb. Caleb. Caleb. Caleb, who was off-limits. Caleb, whom she had no business pining over. *Say yes,* she told herself.

Instead she said, "I don't want to risk coming between you and Kent. He's very protective."

"Oh, he knows," Rick said quickly. "So do your father and Caleb. I would never dream of approaching you without talking to your family, considering the friendship."

Her heart thundered in her ears. For a moment, she was that teen girl with a crush on the boy who didn't want her, on the boy who'd say she was too young. She was so tired of being that girl with Caleb. She'd pined for this man for a ridiculous lifetime only to have him handing her off like a hot potato, once again.

"Caleb?" she asked. "Caleb knew you were asking me out?" She didn't wait for an answer, and she didn't have to for the truth to find her.

She whirled to face the horseshoe area, to zoom in on Caleb, who lazily lounged against the old oak tree. His gaze locked on her with Rick, yet he was too far away for Shay to read him. But she didn't have to. She felt him in every pore of her body, and she didn't want to. Not anymore. She wanted to get him out of her mind, out of her life, out of her head. And damn it, he seemed to think Rick was a good match for her. Maybe she should think so, too. Her chin lifted in defiance, ignoring the pinch of hurt in the center of her chest threatening to expand.

"I didn't mean to upset you," Rick said. "I thought Caleb was like your other brother. Kent said..."

"He is," Shay said, turning her attention back to Rick. "Caleb is my other brother. I'm just not used to him being around anymore." She studied Rick. Damn it, he was good-looking and a nice guy. She was crazy to ignore him. Besides, she needed someone to kiss. Someone who wasn't Caleb. Someone who could knock some sense into her head.

She cast Rick a beaming smile, praying it looked at least a little sincere, and wrapped her arm around his. "Why don't we go inside and see if I can dig you up a shirt to wear that isn't smeared with ranch dip."

His eyes lit up, his hand sliding over hers where it rested on his arm. The small talk started on the walk to the house and she tried to listen. But all she could think about was the tingling sensation of being watched. By him. By Caleb. Probably all too happy right about now. He'd gotten his way. She was walking away with another man.

***

THE INSTANT SHE SLIPPED her arm around Rick's and started marching toward the house, betrayal ripped through Caleb. As if she were one of his fellow Aces, a trusted friend who'd reached over and pulled his weapon from the holster and shot him with it. That was how personal the blow; how bitter the bite. Which was insanity. Shay owed him nothing. He had no rights to her, no claim.

Caleb tipped up his beer and drank. Then he did the same with Rick's. Maybe for the first time in years, he'd get wasted. Completely flipping wasted. He glanced at Sharon, who was now standing with Bob, smiling up at him...oh, so happy. Okay. "Wasted" wasn't an option. At least not here. Not now.

He watched one of Bob's brothers toss a horseshoe. He was a good guy named Mickey, who had always made Caleb feel like genuine, blood-related family. This was his family. Shay was his family. He took another drink. This time the beer was hot and bitter, like the feeling welling inside him.

Kent took another shot and missed. Mickey and Bob cracked jokes. Kent headed toward Caleb. "Go ahead and crack your joke. Get it over with now."

Caleb barely heard Kent, despite Kent getting up close and personal. He was thinking about Shay. About the look on Shay's face just before she'd turned away from him. The defiance etched in her delicate features flashed in Caleb's mind, followed by the image of her walking arm-in-arm with Rick. She was trying to make him jealous. Or trying to spite him.

Caleb glanced at Kent and shoved the beers in his hands. "You've never been a good shot when you're sober. Drink up. I'll go for more."

Before Kent could respond, Caleb started walking, his fingers curling into his palms by his sides. He'd played this cat-and-mouse game with Shay for too long. She could have whatever man she wanted, but not like this, not because of him, to get to him. At least, that's what he told himself so he could ignore the twist of jealousy inside him.

He cut into the house, through the patio door and then ground his teeth when Shay and Rick were nowhere to be seen—and neither was anyone else, for that matter. Everyone was outside, socializing, having fun, allowing Shay the empty house to be with Rick. He crossed the room, possessiveness just beneath the surface, though he preferred to call it protectiveness.

The sound of Shay's laughter fluttered down a hallway—that damn angelic laugh that had driven him wild a good half of his life, now velvety with a distinct hint of flirtation. A few more steps, and a lot more of that protectiveness ground a path along his nerve endings.

The laughter floated closer, along with the soft muffled sound of Shay's voice. Caleb stopped dead in his tracks. The sound was coming from Shay's old bedroom. Oh, hell, no. This wasn't happening. Caleb charged forward, on edge and ready for war. He rounded the corner to the room, door open, to find Rick sitting on Shay's bed.

"Almost ready," Shay called out softly from the closet.

Caleb didn't want to know what she was ready for. Anger spiked inside him. His years of combat were the only thing that kept him outwardly in check when inside he was raging, a distinct tick in his jaw pulsing.

Rick's gaze was riveted to the doorway as if he sensed the crackle suddenly in the air. And apparently he didn't like what he saw in Caleb's face. He paled and jumped to his feet.

"Leave now," Caleb said before Rick could speak, his voice low and even.

Rick was already headed to the door.

"Okay, I found a shirt," Shay said, walking out of the closet. She was still dressed in the cover-up that seemed far more skimpy up close than it had across the lawn.

"Caleb?" she said, surprised. "What's going on? Rick! Wait. You need the shirt."

"Rick was just leaving," Caleb said, ignoring the T-shirt in her hand. "He has his own shirt."

Rick stopped in front of Caleb out of necessity. Caleb was blocking his way. "It's best you call it a day," Caleb said thickly.

"This isn't what it looks like," Rick said. "I—"

"I don't care," Caleb said shortly. "Don't want to know."

"Caleb!" Shay objected. "Stop acting like a brute. Rick, don't go." Rick didn't look at her.

Caleb stepped aside. "Goodbye, Rick."

And just like that, Rick was gone. Shay shoved her hands onto her hips and glared. "What the heck do you think you are doing, Caleb?"

He shut the door, the scent of citrus and honey flaring in his nostrils. Shay's scent, for as long as he could remember. It breathed in the room like a living thing. Just as the lust and tension between them had for far too long now. It was time to deal with it, once and for all.

Caleb leaned against the door, arms in front of his chest, one booted foot over the next. "We need to talk."

3

CALEB COULD SEE the firestorm coming. Shay's eyes darkened and pink rushed across the delicate ivory of her skin—both sure signs she was in fighting mode. He had a knack for bringing it out in her. Had intentionally drawn her right to this hot little spot of temper as he had so many times in the past. As a defense, a distraction. Anything to fight the forbidden, sizzling-hot attraction that had always existed between them.

"Talk," Shay repeated, starting to walk toward him. "I've not heard a word from you in the two months you've been home, and now you want to talk. Because *you're* ready. All the times I was ready, you tucked tail and ran."

"I'm not running now, Shay," he said, not denying the truth. He had run. Run and hoped they'd outgrown the adolescent infatuation they'd shared. But it had matured as they had, turned dangerous in its demand. "I'm here. I'm ready. Let's talk." It was long overdue and he knew it.

"Well, I'm not ready." She stopped in front of him, impatiently waving him aside. "You might as well move away from in front of the door, Caleb. The only person I'm going to talk to right now is Rick. You scared the man half to death with that 'lethal soldier' act of yours. That was rude and it was wrong."

"Rude was visiting the daughter of the party's host in her bedroom," he said. "Rick deserves to be scared."

"*You're* in my room," she pointed out. "What does that say about you?"

"I belong here. Rick doesn't."

"I decide who belongs in my room," she said and held up a finger to stop his objections. "It's still my room, whether I live here or not. And unlike you, Rick was invited." She slapped the shirt in her hand against Caleb's chest, and he reached up and caught it as she added, "He needed a shirt. Too bad I didn't spill my plate on you instead of him."

He started to toss the shirt, and his gaze caught on the University of Texas championship logo. "Wait one damn minute." His eyes jerked to hers. "This is my shirt," he said, then added, incredulously, "You were giving him *my shirt*."

"*My* shirt," she declared, hands on her scantily clad hips.

"That you stole from me the year I moved into this house to sleep in and never gave back. You know damn well you were giving him that shirt to piss me off."

She snatched the shirt right back from him and tossed it over her shoulder. "It was convenient. Like you shoving Rick in my direction because you couldn't handle being in close quarters with me."

"I'd say I'm pretty damn close right now." Close enough to see the sprinkle of light brown freckles on her nose that she hated and he loved. Close enough to touch her. "And I had nothing to do with Rick, besides kicking him out of here. The date thing came from Kent and your father."

She didn't look convinced. "Rick sure didn't see it that way."

"I didn't say I wasn't there when Rick was pining over you," he agreed. "But you know damn well I couldn't say anything without drawing questions."

"Right," she said smartly. "We wouldn't want to draw any questions. Better everyone think we've decided we don't like each other than dare believe we want to jump each other's bones."

"Touchy, touchy," he chided. "See. I knew you were pissed at me. Exactly why I wasn't going to risk you using Rick to get back at me."

"You sure are full of yourself, Caleb Martin," she roared back. "It takes a lot of arrogance to assume I only wanted Rick to get back at you."

"You did just say you wanted to jump my bones," he pointed out, teasing her despite himself. It was second nature, a part of what he'd always done to her, with her. It was also going to get him in deeper water, but then, with Shay, he was damn near always drowning anyway. "I said *we*, not *I*, and I was only making a point and you know it."

"Anger works like alcohol on you," he said. "It makes you say what you really feel. And anger, directed at me, makes you do things you normally wouldn't do. Not only were you giving Rick my shirt, you were alone with him in a bedroom at your conservative parents' house. That's not you and you know it."

Her eyes flashed. "How would you know what is or isn't me, Caleb?" She poked his chest, her body barely a hairbreadth from his. "The few times you came into town over the past ten years, we both hoped we'd have outgrown the past. When we hadn't, instead of dealing with it and talking to me, you avoided me like the plague. Like that somehow made it all go away, but really it was just you that went away. Well, it's not going to work now that you're home, Caleb. Kent, Mom and Dad are going to start asking questions about the tension between us."

Her eyes pierced his, her glare packed with challenge. "And you know what else isn't working? You pretending that dumb ten-year-old kiss didn't happen, and then looking at me like you want to kiss me again. It's ticking me off." She poked his chest again. "Bad."

He wanted to drag her into his arms, every nerve ending in his body aware of her, aware of how long they'd wanted each other, how long they'd denied that need. "I'm not trying to piss you off, Shay."

"Too late," she declared, a tiny lift to her pointed chin, which indicated confrontation, but her hand uncurled beneath his hold and flattened against his. Her voice softened. "Sometimes I just think...maybe...we're like the apple to Adam and Eve. It was just an apple, but the forbidden aspect made it tantalizing. Maybe if we kiss again, we'll find that the first kiss has been blown into something bigger and better than it really was. Maybe then we can just move on."

Whoa. She thought that kiss—the one that had kept him fantasizing for ten flipping years—wasn't as good as they remembered? He must be insane, because the idea wasn't half-bad. He wanted the kiss to be nothing. He wanted the torment of wanting the forbidden fruit to be gone. Then again, a part of him didn't want it gone. It simply wanted her without recourse. Which was impossible.

"It won't work," he said, slipping away from her as if burned. Shay was leaning slightly in his direction, and the action caught her off guard. She swayed into him, her slender body melting against his. She gasped and caught herself with her hands, no doubt a result of her hips pressed against his. He was hard, thick and pulsing with ache. He had been from the moment he'd drawn that first breath of her scent.

His hands went to her shoulders, and Caleb's eyes locked with hers. She wet her lips—nervously, not seductively—but the impact was no less alluring. No less tempting. Suddenly, the kiss held new appeal.

Caleb slid his hands over her shoulders toward her neck, and she shivered beneath his touch. It was the first time he'd ever allowed himself to touch her like a man touches a woman.

"Shay," he said softly, lacing his fingers into the wild mane of blond, pool-tangled locks that framed her heart-shaped face.

She lifted on her toes, closing the distance between her petite five foot two inches and his six-foot frame, bringing their lips close, a breath apart. He could all but taste her. He was going to taste her. Again. Finally.

Until abruptly, a fist pounded on the door behind Caleb. "Shay?" Kent's voice called. "Caleb? You in there? What happened to Rick?"

Caleb reined himself into control instantly, Kent's voice a much-needed cold dose of reality.

Shay's hands went to Caleb's wrists. "No," she whispered. "Not again." She raised her voice. "Go away, Kent!"

"Not until I find out why Rick peeled out of the driveway and won't answer his cell phone."

"No," she said to Caleb. "Not this time. Not until we finish this once and for all."

"Finish what?" Kent demanded through the door.

Shay growled low in her throat, like only a sister can at her brother. "Fighting! We're fighting."

"If you don't open the door," Kent warned, "you can add me to the battleground."

Any minute now, Kent was going to get impatient and reach for the doorknob, which wasn't locked. Caleb reached for Shay and pressed his lips to her ear, trying not to think about her body next to his. "You aren't going to wake up and find out I left tomorrow," he promised. "I'm staying." What that meant for Shay and him, he didn't know, but whatever it was, they had to deal with it, once and for all. Just not now.

He set her back from him before she knew what he was doing and turned the doorknob, allowing Kent's entry. Kent was inside in a heartbeat, and like the previous time ten years ago, Kent's timing had been perfect. He'd once again saved Caleb from a grave mistake. Had Caleb kissed Shay again, he had no doubt it wouldn't have stopped there. Not this time. He wanted her too badly, and Caleb was smart enough to know the line between lovers and enemies was too fine to walk with Shay.

No matter how good she felt, no matter how good she smelled, Shay wasn't the woman for him...no matter how much she always seemed to be that and more.

4

"LET THE TALKING BEGIN," Kent declared, taking up way too much space in Shay's bedroom as far as she was concerned. "What the heck happened to Rick?" he demanded.

With her breath lodged in her throat, Shay's eyes locked on Caleb's face. Her skin was still hot from his touch. But he wasn't looking at her. He was leaning against the wall, arms in front of his chest, focused on Kent.

"Rick had not only found his way into Shay's bedroom," Caleb said, "he was on her bed."

"Caleb, damn it!" she exclaimed. He was trying to draw attention away from the two of them by turning the heat on Rick.

"What?" Kent said, whipping around to Shay. "I thought Rick had more class than that. I might have to kill Rick. And you, Shay. Do you know how upset Mom and Dad would have been if they'd found you in here with him?"

"Oh, good grief," she said, cutting Caleb a hard look. "You two talk this out. I'm going to gather everyone for gifts and cake."

"You come back here!" Kent yelled.

Shay kept walking, but she still heard Kent mumble, "When I told Rick there was no time like the present, I didn't know he was going to try right here and now."

That drew Shay to a halt. She wasn't going to let Rick's friendship with Kent suffer because of her and

Caleb. She started to turn, when she heard Caleb say, "It wasn't like that. Shay was just getting Rick a shirt, but I sent him home before I knew what was going on."

Despite her frustration, which was part emotional, part sexual, Shay felt her lips lift ever so slightly. There was a reason her family had taken Caleb in. He was a man of honor, a born gentleman. She sighed heavily, her breath shuddering from her lungs. Being with her would defy everything he believed in, everything he felt was right. To him, she really was that damned forbidden apple. She didn't want to lose the garden for the fruit any more than he did, but just when he was back—to stay this time—it seemed so was the temptation to see if they could have both.

***

AN HOUR LATER, filled with cake and cheer, a good twenty-five guests—family, friends and neighbors—gathered poolside as Sharon and Bob opened gifts.

All too aware of Caleb sitting not far away in an outdoor chair with a beer in hand he'd hardly touched, Shay stood behind her parents, gathering wrapping paper as it was ripped away and organizing packages.

Shay chuckled as her father, a UT Longhorns season-ticket holder, unwrapped his-and-hers Texas Aggie shirts from a former coworker. The principal of the school where her mother had taught for twenty years gave Shay's father a huge supply of coffee. Knowing how cranky Sharon was without her morning caffeine, it was a gift meant to ensure another happy forty years.

One of the final packages was a large envelope from Caleb. Shay stared at it curiously and, unable to stop herself, cast him a questioning look. He simply smiled and sipped his beer.

"From Caleb," Shay said, handing it to her parents, and looked over her mother's shoulder as the envelope was unsealed. Shay gasped at the same moment her mother did...at the airline tickets and hotel vouchers for a second honeymoon.

"Italy?" Shay silently mouthed to Caleb.

"It's a trip to Italy!" Sharon said to the crowd, who gasped, oohed and aahed. "I've always wanted to go to Italy."

"I remember you saying that every time we went to Olive Garden," Caleb teased.

Everyone laughed. Sharon blushed. "It's because they send their chefs to Italy to train. It's so exciting. The idea of being sent to school in Italy. It makes me want a second career as a chef."

"You can take a class while you're there," Caleb suggested.

Sharon's eyes lit up before she shook her head. "We can't accept this, Caleb. No. It's too extravagant. What about that business you started, the Hotzone?"

"I took several lump-sum, reenlistment bonuses and bought some lucky stock. Enough to leave the Army when the time was right to open the Hotzone. And I set the money aside for your fortieth anniversary years ago."

Kent eyed a brochure for the villa Caleb had rented for his parents. "What the heck kind of stock did you buy, man, and can I get some?"

Caleb leaned back in his chair and set his beer on the ground. "Apple before the Mac craze," he said nonchalantly, as if it weren't a big deal. "I bought in at the right time and stayed in."

"No way," Kent and Bob said in unison. Kent quickly added, "That kind of stuff never happens to me. How much did you net?"

"Kent," Sharon reprimanded sharply, "that's rude. We have company."

"Right," Kent said, elbowing Caleb. "Tell me later."

Caleb laughed and slipped one arm up on the back of his chair, his focus on Sharon and Bob. "This trip is the least I can do to thank you guys, considering you put up with me for so many years."

Shay's heart squeezed at the sweetness of the words that she knew reached deep beyond the gift, into Caleb's soul. She'd never wanted him more than in that moment. And she'd never known just how wrong it was to pursue her interest in him, either. The idea that she'd kept Caleb away from all of this was hard to swallow. But when they were together, things like what happened in that bedroom always happened. The crackling intensity between them had gradually become more like firecrackers than sparklers.

"Son," Bob said, "that's what families do. It's our honor to kick, beat and harass each other, and in turn, to kick anyone to the curb that tries any of the above outside our little unit. The only thing I or Sharon want is more of your time. You need to come out to the house more often."

"When you get back from Italy," Caleb agreed, "I'll eagerly come by to be kicked, beaten and happily harassed."

Kent offered to be lead harasser, and though Shay normally would have volunteered her services as well, she held back. History said the more she teased and played with Caleb, the more their attraction bubbled into demand.

Distracted, she barely registered the final gift—a bottle of wine from their neighbor—until her mother handed it to her.

"That's it," Shay called out and glanced at the sun's rapid decline.

"Poker game starts at seven o'clock," Kent added, rubbing his hands together and elbowing Caleb. "Time to hand over some of that Mac money."

Shay sent Kent a warning look. "Poker is hardly the romantic way to end this day."

"That's what Italy is for," Kent replied. "The way Dad plays poker, he'll have won big, and Mom can spend more on the trip."

"You leave tomorrow," Caleb offered, "so you need to start packing."

Sharon jumped to her feet. "Tomorrow? I can't leave tomorrow. The house is a mess and—"

"I'll clean up," Shay promised. "And you can pack. A little party mess is no reason to miss Italy."

"You're retired," Caleb said. "You can make the short notice. The whole idea is to get whisked away from your party like you would from your wedding."

"I'm game," her father said. "In the meantime, I'll play poker." He kissed Sharon's hand and held it in his. "While you do that packing."

"Bob!" Sharon objected.

"Kent's right," Bob said quickly. "I win on poker night. That means you get to shop more."

"And if you lose?" Sharon asked, propping her free hand on her hip.

Bob winked. "After forty years, you should know I never lose."

Sharon harrumphed. "You always seem to forget that when there's bad luck."

Bob pulled her into his lap. "Because I have a forty-year-old lucky charm."

Shay smiled at the two of them, her gaze lifting and brushing Caleb's—a brush she felt to her toes. They had to talk. But not here, not today. On the phone, where they were a safe distance apart, and she wouldn't become weak. They'd figure out a way to deal with all this tension between them once and for all—and not by kissing. Talking. *Yes,* she silently vowed. *Talking.*

It was her mother that broke the connection, darting to Caleb for a big hug. Her father followed.

When the sentimental interlude ended, Caleb said, "When you get back from Italy, why don't we plan a family outing at the Hotzone? Kent's the only one who's been out to jump. We have a huge grill out there. We can barbecue and make a day of it."

"Oh, yeah," Kent said. "It's a rush you gotta experience to believe."

"Sounds lovely," Sharon said. "As long as I can watch from the ground. That's as close to jumping out of a plane as I'm getting."

"I might just want to try it," Bob said, his eyes lighting up with the idea.

"What about you, Shay?" Caleb asked, surprising her.

"Shay's been taking flying lessons," her father bragged, before she could reply. "She made a list of a hundred things she wanted to do before turning fifty, and her pilot's license is one of her top five to-do items."

"Really," Caleb said. "So flying lessons and what else?"

"It's a hundred items," Shay said, not about to reveal the list that had "finally make love to Caleb" in a high-ranking position. "Too long to detail. But I can assure you that skydiving is not on it. Flying a plane isn't the same as jumping out of a plane. Somehow the two just don't mix." She hesitated a second. "Some things," she added meaningfully, "are just better left alone."

His eyes narrowed. "And sometimes, you just have to jump."

"See now," her father said, "that's the right attitude. Sometimes you just have to jump, Shay. You're always so structured."

"Hush, Bob," Sharon said. "I'm scared enough with her taking flying lessons. That's daring enough for our little girl."

Shay heard her parents, even the outdated "little girl" comment—she was twenty-eight years old, after all. But it was Caleb's words that had her mentally shaking cobwebs from her brain. *Sometimes you just have to jump,* he'd said. The past fluttered through her mind, the times Caleb had been home. When she'd pulled away, he'd pulled her back. When he'd pulled away, as he had today, she'd pulled him back. This was a tug-of-war cycle, and until now, she had never recognized it. She doubted he did because only an hour before, she knew he'd been thankful for Kent's interruption. Now he was pursuing, and he melted her resolve all too easily.

She straightened her spine, trying to get them to the same place at the same time for once. "When you have to push the person out the door, it's better to leave them on the ground."

"You can jump tandem with me," Caleb suggested. "We attach a harness and jump together."

Kent snorted. "She's accident-prone. She might drag you down with her, Caleb."

"I am not accident-prone," she scoffed.

"Think jeans in the oven," Kent teased.

With a growl, Shay grabbed the bottle of wine and moved it to the pile of presents, needing something to do with her hands besides punch her brother. And despite swearing she wouldn't respond to his childish teasing, she couldn't resist an opening when he gave it to her. "That's me. Accident-prone. I can see it now. I'll be attached to Caleb with some fancy harness and the chute won't open. Then we both crash onto the hard ground and die horrific deaths."

"Oh, goodness," Sharon said. "Can we not talk about this? I finally have Caleb home, out of a war zone. I don't want to start thinking about the dangers of any of you crashing to the ground and dying."

"No one is crashing to the ground and dying," Shay assured her. "Caleb knows what he's doing, with the exception of his suggestion that I jump with him. Fortunately, I have enough sanity for both of us. I'm not even considering it." She held the wine up. "I'll go chill this wine in case you want some later." She wiggled a brow. "When you and Dad are alone." She needed a breather away from Caleb, away from watchful eyes.

Shay headed for the house, deeming it time to change clothes now that pool-time was over. Maybe take a quick shower. Walking around half-dressed wasn't helping her avoid Caleb.

Almost instantly though, her nerves tingled, and she knew, even before he spoke, that Caleb had followed. She could feel him. She could always feel him.

"Hold up," he said. "I'll help you." He fell into step beside her as they approached the patio leading to the kitchen.

"What are you doing, Caleb?" she asked softly. "I don't need help chilling a bottle of wine. I thought the idea was to stay away from each other?"

"Funny," he said. "I remember you saying something about Adam and Eve and the forbidden kiss, which I've spent the past hour considering." He reached in front of her and opened the sliding glass door, mischief in his eyes as he waved her forward. "Ladies first."

"There's nothing to consider, Caleb," she said. "You do remember the part of my comparison that made it as insane as me tandem-jumping out of a plane with you? The part where Adam ate the apple and doomed mankind?"

"Fortunately, I doubt we wield power over mankind," he said. "Let's go inside."

She opened her mouth to argue, but realized this was, indeed, a conversation best had inside—away from prying eyes. Shay shoved aside the heavy beige curtain that had been left in place to keep the house cool. A blast of air-conditioning washed over her hot skin and she welcomed it—and not because of the sun. Because Caleb was on her heels, the door already shut behind him. The house was silent but for Caleb's boots clicking on the ceramic tile, warning her there was no escape.

Shay yanked open the fridge and shoved the wine inside. She turned to find Caleb leaning on the kitchen island, a step away. "You're in my personal space," she said. "A good way to get some of that attention you claim you don't want."

"Maybe I want you in my personal space."

"Until someone shows up."

His lips—those full sensual lips—offered a hint of a smile...the "hint" being oh, so sexy. "I know a way around that," he promised.

"Do I dare ask?"

"Better I demonstrated," he assured her. And then, in a flash, he tugged her into the pantry and shut the door. A second later, the impossible happened. Caleb kissed her.

5

HE'D BEEN SEDUCED by watching her beside the pool, eating cake, laughing with family. Being her. That's all Shay had to do to tear down his resolve to stay hands-off, and she'd done it in a mere hour. A pretty quick turnaround unless one considered it had been ten years in the making. And he wasn't giving either of them time to think. They'd done enough of that. Done enough stalling and lusting, and as for himself, he'd had enough time to change his mind—or hers.

She tasted like chocolate icing with a hint of salt and sunshine. Addictive. Perfect. Her tongue was tentative at first, her body stiff. Until she melted—melted like that icing had in the hot Texas sun by the pool. And there was no doubt—this kiss was everything he'd expected and more. This kiss was a kiss that demanded more, because it wasn't just a kiss. It was a doorway to long-suppressed passion. It was the beginning.

Shay knew it, too—he sensed it in her increasing response. The way she lifted to her toes, the way her tongue softly caressed and then reached deeper, seeking more. He slanted his mouth over hers, giving her what she requested. Her reply was a delicate purring sound deep in her throat, barely audible, but so seductive. Her fingers walked up his chest and twined behind his neck, her chest hugging his. Their hips aligned and, yes, he was hard again. A half-naked Shay, kissing him like there was no tomorrow, could have gotten him hard behind enemy lines, under fire.

Instead, they were isolated, in a dark pantry, which was enhancing the sense of taste and touch. He told himself to pull away, to drag her out of the pantry before they were discovered. This was meant to be a quick kiss, the kiss that tore down barriers and took them beyond the "what if?" to "what next?"

She had him vibrating with need. He hesitated. Actually, it was one of his hips vibrating. Like... Shay tore her mouth from his. "Phone," she whispered and reached for her hip, the one resting against his vibrating one.

Okay. Maybe the kiss wasn't as good for her as it was for him, because she was actually planning to answer the call.

Her hand flattened on his chest, and she answered his unspoken worries, as if she sensed his thoughts. "I have my service on a special vibrate alarm. I'm not on call. They wouldn't call unless it's urgent."

Understanding inked into his mind about the same moment she reached for the door. She was about to exit when she leaned back toward him and pointed. "We...we..." Exasperation laced her voice, the darkness shrouding her features. "I don't know what to say."

She opened the door and darted out. Caleb was about to follow when it slammed on him. He grimaced about the time Kent's voice filtered through the air. "We decided to start the poker game early. Where's Caleb? We want his dime involved."

Oh, crap. The poker game was at the kitchen table, the eat-in table by the patio door overlooking the kitchen. Shay wasn't trapped, but he was.

"Where is he?" Kent asked.

"In the pantry," Shay said matter-of-factly.

"Why the heck is he in the pantry?"

"He went in to look for the cookies Mom made for him," she said, and instantly a lightbulb went off in Caleb's mind. He flipped the light on and started looking for the Tupperware container Sharon always hid his cookies in so Kent wouldn't eat them all. He found it on the second shelf and opened the lid.

"That doesn't explain why the door is shut," Kent said, suspicious.

"I shut him in to shut him up. He's a nag, like you. I have to call my service. I have some sort of emergency."

Caleb opened the door with a cookie in his mouth as Shay headed down the hall, phone in hand. "This is Dr. Shay White," she was saying.

Caleb eyed Kent. "Don't even think about touching my cookies."

Kent laughed and walked toward him, determined to snatch a cookie. "You can bet them on a hand of poker."

"Forget it," Caleb said. He'd never been a lucky poker player. The question was, had his gamble with Shay paid off? And how long was it going to be before he could get her alone and find out? He'd come too far to turn back. Soon, he vowed. Tonight, if he had his way. Though it hadn't been planned like that, her parents would be gone for almost two weeks. A perfect time to get the apple off the tree, and then reattach it permanently. He and Shay were going to work off the fascination. It was a better plan than walking around on pins and needles—the only plan he had.

***

IT WAS THIRTY MINUTES after that sultry encounter in the pantry with Caleb, and Shay had showered and changed, and still, her body hummed from his touch, his kiss. Standing in front of the mirror in the bathroom, which was attached to her old room and was well-stocked thanks to her mother, she dried her hair to a sleek finish...and thought about Caleb. Thought about the kiss.

Any hope that kissing Caleb would prove the kiss of the past was nothing but a blown-up memory was gone. Kaput. For the first time ever, it seemed as if she and Caleb might really explore what was between them. And for the first time ever, she realized if it went wrong, the divide between them, and him and the family, could become too much to recover. She was terrified, which was an unexpected reaction to something she'd believed she wanted. But this was real, not fantasy, and there was a lot on the line.

A flashback of Caleb pulling her into the pantry played in her head. Of the feel of his hard body pressed to her. Good gosh, she was a mess. Shay leaned on the sink and turned off the dryer. Her eyes were glossy with the memory, and she could still taste him on her lips, still feel his hands on her body. His hot-and-cold routine had officially reached extreme levels and so had her body's demand for satisfaction. *Hot and cold,* she reminded herself. Whatever got into Caleb in that kitchen wouldn't last. There was no reason to panic. They would put this behind them like they had every other "almost" moment, despite the fact that this time didn't exactly rank as an "almost" worthy event.

Thank goodness a patient had given her an excuse for leaving the party early. Shay stopped at the full-length mirror and sighed. Faded jeans and a *Sex and the City* T-shirt hardly seemed the right attire for an office visit, but she didn't have time for a trip home.

Shoving her purse over her shoulder, she headed for the doorway, remembering the night she and her friend Anna—a doctor who worked in her building—had gone to the *Sex and the City* movie for a girl's night out. Shay had often seen Caleb as her "Mr. Big," the kind of guy you want but never really have. But then, shockingly, during the movie the heroine, Carrie, had gotten her man—and married Big.

Shay had been happy, sad, confused...irrationally bothered by the loss of her Big/Caleb comparison, which had been oddly comforting but no longer existed.

Shay shoved aside her movie reverie as she entered the kitchen and found Caleb, Kent, her father and several other males sitting at the table, the poker game in full swing. The instant her gaze landed on Caleb, her breath lodged in her throat. Fortunately, she was quiet enough to go unnoticed, which allotted her a second to compose herself. That was, until she noticed who was sitting next to her father. With cards in her hand.

"Mom?" Shay asked in surprise. "What's going on? You don't gamble."

"Hey, sweetie," Sharon said, setting her cards face-down and then smacking Bob's hand when he tried to look at them. She smiled at Shay. "Someone has to keep him from losing all our money before Italy." She held up a wineglass. "Have some wine. It's excellent."

The kiss, her mother gambling—had she fallen asleep and woken up in another dimension? Suddenly aware of the warm blanket of Caleb's attention, Shay said, "Can't. I have to go to the office and meet a patient."

"On a Saturday night?" Caleb asked, forcing her to acknowledge him.

"Dressed like that," Kent added, eying her ripped-style jeans.

Irritably, Shay defended herself. "It's all I have with me."

"What in the world is such an emergency that you have to meet the client now?" her father grumbled.

Shay leaned on the island counter. "This client—" she intentionally left out the name for privacy reasons "—lost his wife three years ago in a mugging. The sudden trauma of losing her has created an obsessive-compulsive disorder. Two months ago—"

"Obsessive-compulsive disorder?" Caleb interrupted, his brows dipping. "And you're going to see him alone in a deserted office building? Is there, at least, a guard on duty?"

"It's safe," she answered evasively. "Besides, this client is a kitten. And a kitten who wouldn't harm a mouse for that matter."

"So was Jack the Ripper," Caleb said cynically. "Until they found out he wasn't." He pushed to his feet. "I'm going with you."

"Hey," Kent said, knocking on the table to get Caleb's attention. "We need you in the game."

"You mean you need my money," Caleb corrected, shoving his chair back into place.

"Can't have one without the other," Kent pointed out, but Caleb wasn't paying him any mind. He had his sights on Shay, and he closed the distance between them with a loose-legged swagger.

"Kent White," Sharon scolded, "how about some concern for your sister?" Her gaze shifted to Caleb, her voice softening. "Thank you, Caleb, for looking out for Shay. I worry about her. It's comforting to know you're here for her while we're away."

Feeling the heaviness of Caleb's keen inspection, Shay squeezed her eyes shut in anticipation of what would follow, silently willing her mother not to issue the oh-so-familiar "she needs a man" line. Not to Caleb, not with Caleb involved. But true to form, her mother added, "She needs a man in her life."

"I don't need a man in my life, Mom," she said, her eyes snapping open to find all six-feet-plus of Caleb towering over her. He arched a brow, amusement in his eyes.

Her mother continued to mean well and make things worse. "I just want you to have a man to take care of you, Shay."

Mortified despite having anticipated such a remark, Shay looked away from Caleb. "You take women back twenty years every time you make that statement, Mom."

Several remarks from the males around the table followed, and Sharon banished them all with a wave of her hand. Except for Kent, of course, who waited for silence and said, "If you'd prefer a woman, sis, we are an open-minded family."

"Enough," Bob chided. "I don't want anyone rushing my baby girl to the altar. She has two brothers. You and Caleb. She doesn't need a husband until she is darn good and ready for one."

Shay bit her bottom lip, tension rolling through her at the brotherly reference to Caleb. "On that note," Shay said, "I should take off. I don't want to be late."

Kent turned off the attitude. "You need to learn to say 'no,' Shay." He'd often told her she worked too hard and never lived life. It wasn't a conversation she wanted to have right now. The whole "need a man" one had been enough. "Hurry and get back here."

Shay pretended they were still jesting. "No," she said. "See? I'm practicing on you. No poker for me."

A conversation about how and when to get her parents to the airport the next day followed. Both Kent and Shay lived in central Austin, near their parents, but the airport was a good forty-minute drive south. Since Kent was traveling out of town on business as well, it made sense for him to drive their parents to the airport. And though her parents pointed out that Caleb lived forty-five minutes in the opposite direction of the airport, at the Hotzone facility, he insisted, he, like Shay, would be at the house before they left, to see them off.

Ready to depart, Shay glared at her father. "Don't let Kent keep you up all night. You have a big day tomorrow."

"I'll go to bed," he said. "I'm not gambling on no sleep and risk missing the alarm and a fancy vacation with your mother."

"Then we better get to playing," Kent said, pointing to the cards irritably and then at Caleb. "You hurry your butt back here lickety-split. We have some serious poker to play and not much time."

"No can do," Caleb said. "I'm all Shay's until bedtime. And I have a sunrise jump in the morning."

His words repeated in her mind. *All Shay's.* Until bedtime! Shay gulped as discreetly as she could manage. Though the words were innocent enough to the rest of the group, they packed a solid punch to her.

This was hardly headed toward that talk-from-a-distance conversation she'd planned, and Shay's mind raced for a way out. Turning to him, she said, "This really isn't necessary, Caleb."

His jaw set. "It's necessary."

Shay knew how uncompromising Caleb was when he made up his mind. He'd made up his mind. "Fine," she said. "Let's go."

With no time to spare anyway, she heaved a sigh, murmured a goodbye and turned on her heels. She rushed to the door, Caleb close behind, so close he was at the door, pulling it open before she could. She didn't look at him. She darted to the high wooden porch, humidity thick and restricting, her focus on the sky.

The half-full moon hung low in the horizon, the sky a swirl of blue, gray, orange and yellow. But it was all a haze in her midst. She was actually nervous. With Caleb. It was crazy, and the unsettling sensation sent her rushing down the stairs in flight.

Her car was just to the right of the front door. Caleb's truck was to the left. She had to pause, had to tell him where they were going.

"I'll follow you, so we don't have to come back here and risk getting pulled into the poker game," he said, sparing her the need to figure out what to say.

She dared a look at him. "You don't—"

"I do," he said, his jaw set the way it had been in the kitchen. Strong. Determined. Two words that often defined Caleb.

Shay tugged her keys from her purse. "Stubborn," she added out loud. Another word that often defined Caleb. "You've always been stubborn."

"Determined," he corrected, a slight lift to his mouth.

Shay turned away, afraid he'd notice she was looking at his lips. His full, sexy lips. *Why* did she keep looking at his lips? *Because he kissed you, Shay, and you want him to kiss you again.*

Shay paused at the side of her silver BMW and unlocked the door. The car had been a splurge the year before when her stockbroker fiancé had broken up with her. He'd said she wanted to love him but didn't. After a few weeks of introspection, she'd known he was right. He'd been more buddy than lover. Comfortable. Safe. And not Caleb, though she barely allowed herself to think such a thing.

Nevertheless, the engagement had ended and Shay had bought herself a replacement for love and happiness—the car. Because she'd worked hard and she could survive—all by herself.

Deep in thought, Shay reached for the door handle when suddenly Caleb's hand was there. She'd not heard him approach, or maybe he'd been by her side the whole time. Electricity shot up her arm, and Shay reacted, yanking her arm back.

If he noticed her rapid withdrawal, Caleb didn't react. He opened the door and waved her forward. A gentleman. Nerves subsided ever so slightly as a memory of Caleb repeating his father's words on many occasions skirted through her mind. "Soldiers are men of honor. They know good manners. Until you piss them off. Then they have none, so—"

"Don't piss me off," he finished for her with a grin. "That was my father. He didn't say a lot, but when he did, he was a straight shooter every time."

"Kind of like you," she said appreciatively. "A nice change from Kent's loud mouth. But I guess that's why he does so well in sales. He's always talking."

They both smiled, and the charge in the air thickened into silence. Shay contemplated about ten things she could say to him, but as she raced through ways to turn them into sentences, nothing cohesive came to mind. Nothing overly coherent, for that matter. There was just her, Caleb and a kiss in the pantry.

"I know," he said, as if one of the ten things had come out of her mouth when it had not. "We'll *talk*. Let's take care of your patient first."

Silent understanding settled between them, and she nodded, but nerves fluttered in her chest again. Their game of tug-of-war had worked until now—one saying *yes* while the other said *no*. But Shay was really hungering for *yes*. If they were alone together, she feared she'd be weak, that she'd forget the potential fallout of an intimate connection between them. She'd most definitely kiss him again. And again. And, oh, yes, again.

Shay hurried into the car before she kissed him then.

6

CALEB FOLLOWED Shay to her office building, a white brick structure in the trendy Arboretum area of northwest Austin, surrounded by weeping willows and rows of perfectly manicured bushes. And as if all the privacy the greenery provided wasn't enough of a safety concern, Shay had ignored the parking lot and headed into a garage beneath the building. Pulling his truck to a halt beside her car, Caleb took one look at the dark, vacant parking garage and shoved open his door with a mumbled curse. He stalked toward Shay as she exited her car.

"This is what you call safe?" he demanded. "What this is...is a perfect setup for someone to attack you. You could scream, and no one would hear you."

"Good," she said, slamming her door shut. "What were you thinking, kissing me like that in Mom and Dad's pantry? What if someone would have seen us?" He was a few inches away, and she shoved at his chest. "Don't ever do that to me again."

He gently snatched her hand. "Kiss you or kiss you in the pantry?"

Bypassing a direct answer, she continued her rant—and damn, he'd missed her rants. "You can't just decide to kiss me when you want to kiss me, after ten years of making me feel like crap for kissing you in the first place."

"I'd like to think kissing me made you feel something other than 'like crap.' And for the record, I only did what you suggested. You said you kept thinking we should kiss again and get rid of temptation. And I decided that all the thinking and not doing was what always got us in trouble." He tugged her closer, slid an arm around her waist. "And you didn't kiss me ten years ago. We kissed each other."

"I started it," she said, swallowing against the raspy tone he noted in her voice.

"And I wanted it," he promised her.

"But you never would have kissed me on your own."

"Never is a long time for two people who want each other the way we want each other. We would have ended up here eventually, Shay, even without that first kiss." His hand slid up her back, and he pressed her closer. He lowered his head, slowly bringing his mouth near hers. "There was enough electricity jumping off us today at that party to light up Texas. I spent every second after Kent interrupted us thinking about the forbidden kiss that would have happened had he not shown up. If we don't do something about what's between us, someone is going to notice—if they haven't already."

"We did do something about it," she said, her breath warm on his lips. "We kissed and it solved nothing."

"One kiss isn't a lot of comfort after ten years of anticipation," he said, his lips close to hers. He could almost taste her now. "Maybe we need to kiss again."

She leaned into him and then suddenly pulled back. "Stop. No." Abruptly, she pushed away from him. "We need to *talk*. You said we'd talk, and I'm holding you to it. And not when I have a client about to show up. I have to be focused on my patient...not on kissing you, Caleb."

"All right then," he said softly, his fingers curling into his palms as he resisted the urge to reach for her again. Now that he had touched her, he wanted to touch her again. Just as he wanted to kiss her again, to tear away the barriers and her clothes, so there was only the passion. It had to be. It would be. "But it's time we deal with this, Shay."

Her eyes went wide. "*Deal with this?* Gee, Caleb. You really know how to steal a girl's heart." She paled instantly. "Not that I mean—" She flung her hands in the air. "We need to go upstairs before my patient arrives. You'll scare the crap out of him, too." She turned on her heels and stomped away.

Caleb ran a hand over his jaw, the light shadow of a new beard rough against his hand. He considered himself a fairly sensitive guy, the front man for missions that had required diplomacy, but it seemed, with Shay, he had a knack for opening his mouth and inserting his foot. Ah, well. Hell, at least that gave him an excuse to keep his mouth occupied in other ways.

With all the ways he might occupy said mouth on his mind, Caleb followed her, a man stalking his prey. Shay's every move attracted his attention. Her every word interested him. Caleb had never felt this way for any other woman. He had every intention of showing Shay exactly how he intended to deal with this "thing" between them.

Shay had been right. Temptation and desire were making them crazy. Him crazy. And it had separated him from the family, forced him to distance himself for fear he would destroy his family bond, when that action itself had darn near done exactly that. That was the lightbulb that had set him into action. They had to put the temptation behind them. And no matter how many times he kissed her, it would simply not be enough to do the job.

***

SHAY PUNCHED the elevator button, waiting, all too aware of Caleb behind her. Close. Too close. Not close enough. She was all over the board when it came to him. She wanted him. She didn't want him. She had thought the kiss was a good idea. Now it felt like a horrible idea.

The doors opened and she stepped inside, pushing the button for the fourth—and top—floor, and faced forward. Caleb stepped in beside her, taking up more space with his sexual energy than any one man should fill. They were alone, the steel doors closing them inside the tiny compartment. And damn him, he smelled good. And tasted good. And felt good. If she looked at him, if she saw the sizzling warm heat of his welcoming stare, she'd forget herself and kiss him. Again.

Memories of their hot and cold moments, as early as today, shuddered through Shay with a deep breath. Caleb could turn off the heat in a snap of his fingers and turn on the silence and withdrawal just as quickly. She knew this. She'd seen this. She even understood it.

True, he'd never before shifted back and forth in this extreme fashion, but he'd shifted plenty. He'd catch himself, check himself. Which meant, no matter how tempting, Shay could not allow anything more to happen between them tonight. Not if she wanted to be sure they could salvage their relationship when this night passed. If she were smart, she'd tell him she was seeing someone else. Tell him she was in love. Set him free. But considering she'd suggested the kiss to end temptation, she doubted she'd be convincing.

The minute the elevator dinged and the doors opened, Shay darted forward, reaching for her purse, which she didn't have. "Oh, no," she said, turning and running into Caleb. Her hands flattened on his chest, her breath lodged in her throat.

"Hello to you, too," he said, his hands on her arms, his thighs—those muscles hugged by denim—touching hers.

Shay shoved out of his arms. "I forgot my keys and purse. Oh, God. And my cell phone, too. They're in the car."

He paused and then said, "It's locked, isn't it?"

She nodded, frustrated at herself for doing something so irresponsible. "And it's your fault, Caleb. I was flustered over you. And now my client is going to be here and I can't get into my off—"

He moving so quickly, she had no warning—just suddenly, his hands were framing her face, his lips brushing hers. A gentle, lingering caress, his warm breath mingling with hers, his tongue just barely slipping past her teeth.

Overwhelmed by the warm awareness spreading across her chest, between her thighs, she couldn't move, couldn't react.

Slowly he pulled back and ran a thumb over her cheek, a slight smile on his oh-so-kissable lips that only made her want to press her mouth to his again. "I figured if I was going to take the blame for all of this, I should get a few of the benefits, as well," he said softly. "And kissing you is definitely a bonus." He slid his hand over hers. "Let's go see what we're dealing with to get your purse." He headed to the stairs with her in tow, and she was still a bit dazed and confused by how easily he'd melted her resolve.

The fact that his hand was big and warm didn't help matters. Nor did the fact that she couldn't help but notice his nice tight backside in those faded jeans. The view was good and she was human. And weak, she chided herself.

Shay snapped her attention upward, refusing to look at his nice tight backside one second longer. Instead, she opened her mouth to chide him as she had herself, to say a few precise words that would disconnect her from the wildfire he'd set off inside her. But she couldn't find even one witty word to keep him away. It had to be the jeans. There was no other explanation. At least, not one she wanted to consider.

Of course, it wasn't long until she had more to consider than the way Caleb's jeans fit. They stood by her car, and Caleb inspected the door. "Nice car," he commented. "I didn't take you for a silver kind of girl, though. Maybe blue."

Shay hugged herself. Caleb knew her so well, it was frightening. "Blue was on back order. It was a splurge, and I was afraid I'd talk myself out of it if I waited. Can you open it?"

"Not a chance," he said without a dash of hesitation. "Not without damage. You got a spare key at home?"

"Spare is at the bottom of Lake Travis," she said. "It's not a good story, but Kent and his boat are involved."

"Ah, yes," Caleb said. "One of Kent's boat parties. Always...interesting. I'm surprised he got you out there."

"I went to pick him up," she said, telling the story despite her intention not to. "He didn't want to drive. Said he'd had too many beers. Of course, that ride wasn't possible since he decided to play football with my keys right by the water."

"Ouch," Caleb said. "I can only imagine the hurting you put on him the next morning."

"I can't blame him this time, though, can I?"

"Just me," Caleb reminded her.

"Well, that's true," she agreed readily. "But we'll talk about that later. Right now, I'm worried about my patient arriving and the fact that I can't get into my office." She frowned and eyed the dainty diamond watch her parents had given her for her twenty-fifth birthday, one of the only pieces of jewelry she owned. "He should have been here by now. George isn't the kind of person who shows up late. Not by a minute." Worry knotted in her chest. "Can I use your phone to call my service?"

He relaxed against the side of his truck, snatched his phone off his belt and handed her a BlackBerry. Shay hesitated before making her call, feeling stuck between a rock and a hard place. "I have to have a phone number where my service can reach me. Can I give them your number until I can swing by a store and pick up a temporary phone?"

"Just keep my phone until tomorrow," he said. "You can give it back when we meet up at the house to see your parents off. By then, we'll have your keys, and phone, in hand."

"What if you need your phone?"

"I'm not a doctor," he said. "And I don't mind."

Reluctantly, she agreed, and a few minutes later, Shay hung up with her answering service and dialed the number they'd given her for George, then updated Caleb. "He didn't call to cancel. I'm really worried now. He hasn't shown up, yet he was desperate to reach me. This isn't like him."

"Maybe the service screwed up," Caleb offered. "Lost a call."

"Maybe," she said, hoping he was right. George's phone rang three times before his answering machine picked up. Shay covered the phone. Using Caleb's phone number for her service and handing out his number to patients were two different things. "Can I leave this number for the patient directly?"

"Anything to help," he said, and Shay felt a flutter in her stomach. He meant it. Anything. He was that kind of person. Always had been. It wasn't that he had kissed her or wanted to kiss her again. It was just Caleb.

Shay left a message on George's phone. "I have a really bad feeling about my patient." She fisted her hand at her belly. "Right here. A knot. I have his address on my laptop at home. I need to go get that and stop by and check on him." Then she eyed her car. "Of course, I can't drive anywhere, and I don't have keys to get into my house. And the dealership is going to be closed." She pressed her hand to her forehead. "Great."

Caleb reached for her and gently pulled her against him. "But you have me."

"Caleb," she said, her hands settling on his arms, fully intending to chide him for the intimacy he was creating, but knowing it wouldn't be convincing even to her own ears. The truth was, this wasn't the first time Caleb's quiet strength and cool sensibilities had calmed her frazzled nerves. He had a way of bringing her down a notch, while Kent—bless her brother's loving heart—had a way of taking her up a notch.

"Your house, I can get into," Caleb assured her. "And I can take you to pick up a key at the dealership tomorrow, either before or after we go see your parents off. As for going by your patient's house, it seems smarter to have the police check in."

She shook her head in rejection. "I can't do that," she said. "If nothing is wrong, he'll feel I've betrayed his confidence, invaded his privacy. I'll lose the ability to help him."

"Does he live in an apartment?" he asked. "The leasing office could check on him."

Her brows dipped. "I don't know, but that's a great idea. We could...I mean I..." It was so easy to use that word—*we*. They'd been *we* many times growing up. Another kiss and suddenly she was questioning if it was okay to use that word.

She stepped away from his arms. "We should go." We. She'd said *we* again.

"Yes," he said softly, holding on to her hand despite her step backward, bringing her hand to his lips. "We should go." He dropped her hand and held open the door.

Soon they were in the truck together, and Shay felt the crackling awareness that had lived between them for so many years shift and change to a relaxed intimacy. She wasn't going to kid herself. She wanted him. If he pushed her hard enough—heck, if he pushed her at all—she'd be naked with him in two seconds flat. So she set her resolve on one small goal. Don't get naked with him tonight. Give him until tomorrow, when she was sure his cold feet would kick in.

7

"THAT TOOK YOU ALL of two minutes."

"Try two seconds," Caleb said, pushing to his feet and opening the door of Shay's house, a redbrick, one-story number, not more than a mile from her office. "Why don't you have dead bolts?"

"They were supposed to be installed as part of the deal when I bought the place six months ago," she said. "When they weren't, I was so excited about finally having my student loans paid off and actually being able to buy a place, that I let it go." She flipped on the light. "But after seeing how fast you can get in, I'm officially moving dead bolts to the top of my 'things to do' list." Shay motioned him inside.

Caleb followed her, his boots scraping glossy, light-oak hardwood. "A locksmith is expensive," he said. "I can do what you need to have done. And I'll make sure I check the whole place for safety. Doors and windows."

"I'd say you don't have to do that," she said, "but I know you. You've made up your mind. You're going to do it." With a lift of her chin, she indicated the room to her left, a kitchen of rich redwood and gray granite counters. "Plenty of Dr Pepper in the fridge. I'll just be in the other room looking up that address." She sashayed her sweet, heart-shaped ass down a short stairwell, leaving him in the midst of a chuckle. He hated Dr Pepper, and she knew it.

Caleb took a step toward the stairs, when his eyes caught on the photo hanging above the rectangular decorative table. He remembered perfectly when the picture was taken. It was "the" day. Shay's eighteenth birthday. Family and a dozen or so friends had gathered at Shay's favorite Mexican-food joint to celebrate, and they'd hijacked the waiter to take a picture. Chairs were scooted close, arms draped shoulders, memories were documented.

And there he was, sitting next to Shay, in all her birthday glow, a smile on her lips as she looked at him, not the camera. And he was looking at her, too, oblivious to the rest of the group. The picture said a million words. They were in private conversation; the connection between Shay and him—the attraction—all too evident. It had been one of two big scares with Shay. The other had been at her college graduation dinner, another milestone in her life that had almost turned into another kiss. He hadn't come home much after that. Even before the kiss they'd shared, he'd known what was between them. And he'd known it was only a matter of time before everyone else would know, too.

After ten years and thousands of miles behind them, that still appeared to be true. But they'd been kids then, young and incapable of maturely handling such circumstances. They weren't kids anymore.

"Caleb!" Shay called. "You have a phone call."

With one last glance at the picture, Caleb headed down the stairs to find a living area washed in the same warm feeling that was Shay, with a large, modern-looking stone fireplace as the centerpiece and a plasma TV mounted on the wall above—perfect for the UT football he'd missed too much of the past ten years. The couch was brown, as was the matching chair and ottoman, both decorated with light blue and brown throw pillows. Light blue candles. Brown picture frames. This was a home.

She held out the phone over the marble coffee table, where she'd set her laptop. Caleb didn't miss the strained look on her face even before she said, "Jennifer."

Somehow Caleb managed not to smile, and quickly reined in a moment of male satisfaction in which his ego screamed, hey-ho-yeah, baby, she was jealous. He'd felt that same pang of the green-eyed monster with Rick, and it was nice to know he wasn't alone.

Caleb accepted the phone, his fingers brushing Shay's on purpose. She snatched her hand back, and this time, he had to turn away to hide a smile.

"What's up, Jennifer?" he asked, walking to Shay's window and pulling up the wooden blinds to inspect her locks. Check. Need replacing.

Jennifer didn't bother with a greeting. "Who the heck was that, and why don't we know about her? I can't imagine you ever letting a woman answer your phone. You're too private. Which means she isn't someone you just met."

"We" meaning her and her husband, Bobby Evans, one of his best friends, a fellow Ace and, now, a business partner. "And your next question would be what?" Caleb asked, redirecting the conversation.

"Check," she said. "You can't talk or don't want to. Fine. But expect the question again. I demand to know the scoop."

"I'd expect nothing less from you," Caleb assured her. He liked Jennifer. And he liked her with Bobby, who was the happiest he'd ever seen the man.

"Good," she said, her tone saying he'd successfully dodged her question. For now. And just to be sure he got the "for now" part, she added, "Then we agree you'll tell me about her later." She didn't give him time to argue. "Onward to the reason I called. We're grilling burgers out at the Hotzone. So we borrowed a few things from your fridge. Mustard, pickles. A few things we forgot."

His place was a small trailer at the back of the facility, meant to be temporary and offering him zero in privacy. "My place is your place. Since you asked and all."

She laughed. "I knew you'd see it that way. I'll save you a burger. Or you could head back now and bring whomever she is with you."

Caleb turned to find Shay scribbling an address on a piece of paper. "Tonight's not good," he replied.

Shay's gaze snapped to his. "It's okay. I'm fine. I can deal with this myself."

He held her stare and said to Jennifer, "Don't keep Bobby up too late. We have a sunrise jump." Shay's eyes went wide before she looked away, although he saw the pink flush of her cheeks first.

Caleb ended the call. "Her husband, Bobby, is one of my partners."

She bit her bottom lip and nodded. "Yeah. I guessed that."

"There is no one else, Shay. Just you."

Instantly, the air thickened with tension. "You didn't have to tell me that."

"And you?" he asked, muscles clenching in his back as he waited for the reply. The idea that she might be seeing someone else hit him with a punch. "Are you seeing anyone, Shay?"

Her lashes lowered, then lifted tentatively. "If I say yes?"

A rush of possessiveness filled him. "I'd say he must not be too compelling since you were in your parents' pantry kissing me."

She blinked and then laughed. "I believe your ego has expanded while you were off becoming some sort of super soldier, able to break into houses with a snap of your fingers."

Caleb wasn't laughing. He was thinking of the illogical dread he'd felt for that day when he might hear she was married. Relief would have been logical—if he didn't really want her. But he did. He always had.

"Answer, Shay," he ordered softly.

Shay turned serious. "No," she said. "I'm not seeing anyone." She firmed her lips. "Including you."

Satisfaction filled him. They'd see about that before this night was over.

***

"THIS IS IT," Shay said, pointing out a stucco-style house nestled in the expensive West Austin area, with lots of trees and hills surrounding it. "I don't see a car, unless it's in the garage, but it looks like there are lights on in the house."

"Didn't you say this guy is a schoolteacher?" Caleb asked, as he pulled into the driveway. "Because teachers don't make this kind of dime."

"He's written some textbooks," she said. "Maybe that pays well. We've never really talked about his financial position." Which, now that she thought about it, he seemed to steer away from in their sessions.

"I doubt that," Caleb said, and eyed the house. "Let's go see good ol' George."

He reached for the truck door, and Shay grabbed his arm. "No. I should go alone. I don't want him to feel

I've betrayed his trust by letting someone else know that he's a patient."

"He'll see me in the truck," he said.

"And I'll tell him you are a friend who knows nothing," she said. "But if you hear me talk with him, that won't play true. Seriously, Caleb. Talking about a case without a name is much different ethically than putting a face to the case. I need to do this alone."

His jaw clenched visibly despite the darkness of the cab. "Don't go inside."

"All right," she said and reached for her door.

Caleb shackled her arm. "I mean it, Shay. Don't go in or I'll come in after you. You never know what someone is capable of, especially someone already unstable."

Shay should have been irritated, but she wasn't. He'd done a lot for her tonight, and she liked feeling cared about. Still, she had to give him a hard time. "Are all soldiers this paranoid or is this a special quality you've honed all on your own?"

"I'm cautious," he said. "But that's not why I'm stopping you now." He motioned to the window.

Shay frowned and followed his direction, gaping at what she saw. In the upstairs window, a couple had appeared, or rather the silhouette of a naked couple.

"He stood me up to have sex," she gasped.

"Looks like," Caleb responded. "In the man's defense, though, you did say he's been reclusive for the three years since his wife died. If this woman showed up and made him an offer while he was in that kind of deprived state, he was probably pretty powerless to say no."

"Hold on a minute. 'I need to make a phone call' sounds pretty simple to me," she said smartly.

He laughed and started the engine. "I say Mexican food and margaritas are in order."

Shay sighed and said, "Yes. Please." She was beyond denying herself time with Caleb. She enjoyed him. She wanted to hear about the last ten years. And they needed to talk. In public, if not on the phone. *In public* being the operative phrase here. That meant she could maintain her "hands off for the night" decision, no matter how hot it might get between her and Caleb. It was a safe plan—she was sure of it.

8

AN HOUR LATER, AFTER George's scandalous window show, Shay sat in a booth across from Caleb in the far dark corner of a hole-in-the-wall Mexican-food joint. A bit off the beaten path, Jose's had less traffic than the busy restaurant scene of Austin on a Saturday night. And darn, was it underrated—both in atmosphere and quality.

Shay ran her hand over her midsection as the waiter took her plate. Her stomach was officially full and happy, and it cared not a bit about the old, scuffed hardwood or the red, weathered booth with a rip here and there. But then, Caleb was enough visual for Shay. The urge to reach over and caress the light stubble dusting his jaw had all but won out at least three times. Four. Right now was four.

She curled her fingers in her lap and quickly distracted herself with another memory—one of many they'd shared over dinner. "Remember the fake ID debacle?"

He paused, beer near his lips. "You mean when Kent tried to sneak into the horse races with an ID that said he was twenty-five, when he was sixteen with peach fuzz?" He chuckled and took his drink.

"Wait," Shay said, leaning forward, flattening her hands on the table. "There was more than one ID debacle?"

"Not if you don't know about it," he laughed and set his beer aside, before adding, "Kent almost talked me into going to the track that day. Said he'd dreamed about a horse's number. We'd be rich. Man almighty, I was glad I didn't get sucked into that little fantasy. He didn't see the light of day for a month, your parents were so angry."

"And he made our lives miserable for it," she said, curling her legs to the side on the booth, one elbow on the white laminate tabletop.

"Yeah," he said, and seemed to be thinking back in time before he laughed again. "Yeah, he really did. But those were some good times. Kent and I...we didn't talk much while I was away, but we're good now. Just like I was never gone. Last Saturday he slept out at the Hotzone so he could do my Sunday sunrise jump with me."

"Mom is beside herself that you're staying in that beat-up trailer rather than with them, you know. I told her you had reasons." She made an uncomfortable sound. "I didn't mention the 'reasons' were all about avoiding me."

"It's not about avoiding you, and the trailer isn't as bad as I'm sure Kent has made it sound," he said. "I'm officially the only one of the three Hotzone owners who's still single. Bobby and Ryan both got themselves married up. I'm the logical Ace to take some of the extra workload. And living on-site helps. They'd do it for me if it were reversed, and one day I'll need time off, and they'll cover for me. We're blood brothers. We've all saved each other's lives more times than I can count."

Shay sobered sharply on the mix of the tequila she sucked through her straw and the words *saved each other's lives*. Her throat constricted, and she barely kept from choking. Shay sat up straight, shoved away the drink, then hoarsely confessed, "I worried about you. I worried a lot."

His expression softened, his eyes gently touching hers. "Shay..."

He reached for her hand, and she pulled back, fiddling with the napkin in her lap. She didn't want to get emotional. She hadn't expected to get emotional. But here were the emotions, overtaking her, demanding notice. And the words—his, and now hers—that seemed to flow of their own accord. "The thought of something happening to you, and then not only losing you, but knowing it was because I'd pushed you away—it ate me alive, especially that first year you were gone. After that, I learned to tuck it away, but there were times, especially after you came home to visit and left again—not that you did that all that often—but after a visit, it would start again. The fear of the phone ringing with bad news. Mom felt it. Dad and Kent, too, but they're too tough to admit it."

He sat completely still for several seconds, so still she wasn't sure he even breathed. And she was pretty sure she'd hit that button—the hot-cold button. The one where he withdrew, where they went back to the not-talking thing they did so well.

And then suddenly, he was beside her, in the booth facing her, his expression etched with tenderness...and something that almost resembled guilt. "I should have talked to you before I left. I should have made sure you didn't feel that kind of fear and guilt. You didn't run me off, Shay. The Army was in my blood—I knew *that* before I started college and I knew afterward. I always knew it was where I belonged."

But not with her, she thought, not with her family. "Then why are you here now? Why did you even come home?"

He hesitated. "Shay—"

His hesitation said everything. "Because you didn't have a choice," she said tightly, turning to face him fully, arm on the table, back to the wall. "Something happened. Something that forced you out."

His lips thinned, telling her before his words that she wasn't going to like his answer. "If I hadn't been ready to get out," he said, "I wouldn't have."

"What happened?" she asked tightly.

"Yes, there was an issue. I helped bring a corrupt person to justice. Something I couldn't do when he had the ability to influence my missions. I could have transferred, but the Flying Aces—my unit—was *it* for me."

Why was this bothering her? Had she really believed in some far off corner of her mind that he'd come back for her? It was silly, but it was there, a part of her subconscious that had whipped its ugly, irrational head into full view.

She turned toward the table, and he took her hand, stalling her movement. But she didn't give him time to say whatever he was going to say. "Months and months would pass, and we had no idea if you were alive." Eight long months the year before last. "I hate you for making me worry. Us. Making us worry."

"I'm sorry." His fingers brushed her jaw, a gentle caress that sent chills down her spine. "I'm here now," he said. "I could have gone anywhere in the world, but I'm here. And I'm not going anywhere, Shay." He laced his fingers with hers. "And I'm done hiding from a kiss. We were kids when it happened. And I believed, back then, if we'd pursued something more, we would have done nothing but destroy each other—and our family—in the process. We had everything to lose by acting on our attraction." He brought her knuckles to his lips. "But we're not kids anymore."

"And yet so little has changed," she said.

"Hasn't it?"

The jukebox started playing a soft Keith Urban tune. He smiled. "Let's dance." And before she could reply, he tugged her forward.

"Dance?" she murmured, looking for a dance floor she'd missed. Where the heck were they going to dance?

The answer was soon evident as he drew her to a halt in the dimly lit deserted corner just beyond the jukebox and a vacant pool table. A good ways from the few lone pool players at a distant table.

His hands settled on her waist. Firm. Possessive. Strong. Objections faded on her tongue, the words of the song that had enticed them to the dance floor forgotten. In their place, other reasons hummed through her mind, explaining why this dance was okay. They were in public. There were people nearby. A dance was a moment in time in the broad picture of things.

But as the stark desire in his expression mingled with the heady male scent of him, which invaded her senses, seducing her, a spell overcame her—a spell where reason didn't breathe, let alone live. A spell that expanded in time, yet felt like only a split second—a second gone too fast.

They stood there, unmoving, staring at one another. His hand slid to her back, gently urging her closer. Their legs aligned, then entwined, intimately placing her hips against his. Shay swallowed hard at the instant heat swirling low in her stomach, and her gaze dropped to his chest, to where her hands rested.

Slowly, her fingers splayed wide on the hard muscle. This was happening. She was touching him, was with him, in his arms, and neither of them was saying no. It was so surreal—it was almost an out-of-body experience. Except her body most definitely wanted in on this action.

Shay slowly slid her hands upward, his body heat warming her palms, and her gaze lifted to his. Her fingers laced at his neck, her chest naturally arching more intimately into his. Their bodies began to sway, the song—another song—slow still, filling the air, but she didn't hear the words. Shay didn't see the room. But neither could she maintain their stare, not when the intensity of what he did to her was downright unnerving.

Shay pressed her head to his chest, heard the rapid beat of his heart, as surely as she felt the hard ridge of his erection pressed against her stomach. He was right. They weren't kids anymore. Everything had changed.

His hands traveled around her back, caressing, before resettling at her waist, his touch possessive and strong, his fingers sensually trailed her ribs, just below her breasts. Driving her crazy with anticipation of where they might travel. Shay pressed her hands then over his at her waist. Squeezed her eyes shut at the tightening of her nipples, the desire willing her to direct his hands where she wanted them. Not caring where they were. Ten years of foreplay apparently had consequences. She'd never felt so erotically charged and lost—not in private, let alone in public. And with what little reason she had remaining, Shay knew she had to end this, to get out of here before she did something she would regret.

Her gaze lifted to his, a plea meant to say, *no more. Stop.* "Caleb," she whispered, and the word was again a plea, but not the one intended. This was a plea for something else, a plea for more of him. A plea that had her pressing to her toes, stretching for his mouth. A plea he answered.

Caleb's fingers slid into her hair, his mouth lowering, a brush of lips, innocent enough for public display until it wasn't innocent at all. Shay had no idea what happened, hardly remembered anything except the burn for more. More of him.

One minute they were on the dance floor. The next she was in the corner, hidden by the jukebox, back against the wall, and Caleb was kissing her. She was kissing him. Wild passionate kissing. Her leg was wrapped around his, her hand in his hair. His hand curved over her backside and pulled her tight against his hips, settling the hardness of him into the *V* of her body. Shay moaned into his mouth at the feel of the thick bulge of his erection. At the feel of his hand finally on her breast. Her hand on top of his telling him not to stop. But he did stop—tore his mouth from hers—and she whimpered from the loss. He framed her face with his hands, stared at her a long, hard moment and then moaned at whatever he saw in her face—the unmasked passion she knew was there. And then he kissed her again. *Yes, more.* But it was short, passionate—over too soon.

He grabbed her hand. "Let's get out of here."

She tried to pull against him, her body screaming in demand. *No. Stay. Kiss. Touch.* But he was strong, insistent, and she followed, rounding the jukebox, and she blinked reality back into view. Heat rushed across her cheeks. There was a pool game going on at the far end of the room. People nearby. And she hadn't cared, and wasn't sure she would care if Caleb pulled her right back behind that jukebox. She barely recognized herself; she'd never be so daring.

Her head was still spinning when Caleb opened the truck door and kissed her quickly—but no less passionately—before helping her climb into the cab. Darkness surrounded her, anticipation of what came next. A tiny sliver of reason said, *Not tonight—he'll wake up with regrets and so will you.* But Caleb was already climbing inside the truck, and all she could think of was how close he was, and how easy it would be to touch him again. How much she wanted to.

He stared out the window but didn't start the engine. He sat there. She sat there. Sexual energy clawed at her, at them, expanding until she thought the windows would burst. And then, he slid the keys into the ignition and started the engine. When he paused, she thought he'd changed his mind, but he reached for her and pulled her to his side, their legs aligned. Her hand on his thigh.

His fingers wrapped around her neck, and he pressed his forehead to hers. "In case you start thinking too much. We're done thinking."

And then he put the truck in gear.

9

WITH ONLY A SHORT one-mile drive from the restaurant to Shay's house, the sexual tension still ran plenty thick between them, and Caleb intended to keep it that way. No more thinking. No more wondering. He killed the engine in the driveway of her house, and before she had time to react, he turned to her, pulled her into his arms and kissed her. There was no way he was leaving her tonight. Whatever was, or wasn't, between them...it was time to find out.

He claimed her mouth with possessiveness, hot and firm, leaving no room for argument. And for a fraction of a second, she hesitated in her response, then moaned, sinking into the kiss. He eased his demand into a slow, sensual dance of tongue against tongue. Savoring her. Savoring the night. Not concerned if he slept, not when Shay was finally in his arms.

Her taste seduced him, climbed inside him and awakened something he didn't know existed. A place where sex wasn't just a destination, where you visited and departed, or an escape from a jungle in some hellhole. It felt like an emotional need. She felt like an emotional need.

"Caleb," Shay whispered against his lips, her fingers pressing into his chest, as if she wanted to push him away but instead absorbed him. His lips brushed hers again, and she breathed, "Wait."

But he didn't wait, because he felt her tension, could almost hear her thinking, finding reasons—as they both had a million times before—to pull back. To leave this "thing" between them—whatever it was—untouched.

Caleb deepened the kiss, his hand sliding up her back and molding the lush curves of her breasts against his chest. Holding her, touching her, his body pulsed with need, his cock thick with demand. He wanted inside her, wanted it as much as he wanted his next breath. But not as much as he wanted to take his time, as he wanted to enjoy every last second of this first time with Shay. And he wanted her to enjoy it, wanted to make her forget to worry.

His tongue glided deeply into her mouth, stroked and prodded with the reminder of how good they felt together, with the promise that he could wash away more than her objections, but also her fears. He was rewarded with another of her soft moans—damn, he really loved those moans. He wanted her more than he remembered ever wanting anyone in his life. Hell, he felt like he'd wanted her his entire life.

His hand stroked the silky strands of her floral-scented hair. "Let's go inside," he murmured, already opening the door and gently dragging her across the seat with him.

But she didn't go willingly. "No, wait," Shay objected again, latching a hand onto the steering wheel to halt her progress. "We can't go back once we do this."

"Good," he said firmly. "I don't want to go backward."

"But we—"

He framed her face with his hands, cutting her words off with actions, pinning her in a stare and a firm but gentle demand. "Do you want me?"

"That's not the—"

"Do you want me?" he repeated softly.

“You know I do,” she whispered.

“And I want you. Very much, Shay.”

A tormented expression touched her face. “Until tomorrow morning.”

“Again tomorrow morning,” he promised. “You can say what you will about temptation and forbidden fruit, but it’s been ten years, and we’re still here, better and hotter than ever. That means something, Shay.” He brushed his thumbs over her cheeks, emotion welling in his chest. “And ten years ago, I walked away because I had to. It wasn’t our time. We were too young. We would have crashed and burned. But it’s our time now, Shay. Here. Tonight.”

One second. Two. Her chin lifted in a familiar, defiant motion. “That’s not what you said this afternoon.”

“I was doing what we’ve both been programmed to do. Run from our attraction. The same way I’m programmed to hear gunfire without flinching. We’re both programmed to see each other and go into avoidance mode.” His hands settled on her legs, his voice deepened into a confession. “The minute I saw you today, I knew I’d stayed away because it was the only way I’d resist you. Then you came in, offering me a kiss. I was trying everything I could to maintain control.” He brushed his knuckles over her cheek. “We both need resolution. We both need to know why we can’t let this go.

“There were times over the past ten years when I was in places as close to hell as it gets. Hurt. Running for my life. Certain I wouldn’t make it. I needed something to cling to that was good. Something that gave me hope. Today, when I was watching you by the pool, helping your mother unwrap gifts, you were smiling and laughing, and I remembered what that good thing was. It was you, Shay. I'd picture your smile...your laugh." His lips lifted slightly, his hand slid to her cheek. "Your dagger-throwing, angry stare when you wanted to kill me. All that means something, and I want to know what."

Her hand went to his wrist, her voice crackling with emotion. "Me? You thought of me?"

"More times than you can possibly imagine," he said. Now that he'd unraveled this web, he wasn't going to tangle it with unspoken words. He'd spent ten years holding back. No more.

She touched his face, fingers trailing over his jaw. "Let's go inside."

***

SHAY TRIED TO OPEN her door, but her normally steady hand shook with the effort. Caleb said something behind her, but she couldn't focus for the thunder of her heart in her chest, radiating into her ears. Couldn't think for the musky, male scent so uniquely Caleb, lifting in the humid night air and thickening. To say that she was terrified she might be making the wrong choice by acting on her desire for Caleb was an understatement. She was scared to say yes to tonight with Caleb, and scared to say no.

Caleb reached around her and took her key. Helplessly, she accepted the aid and fought the urge to lean back on him. That leaning on him felt safe said a lot. Her parents had taught her to be strong and independent, to lean on those you trust, and be picky about who was inside that circle. Caleb was in that circle. No other man ever had been. He'd seen her strong, seen her weak. Heck, he'd tended to her annual stomach flu when she'd been death warmed over.

Caleb's lips brushed her neck, and she realized she was doing more than thinking about leaning on him. She *was* leaning on him, her body resting against his bigger, harder one. He'd known she needed a minute, known not to push her.

Caleb turned the doorknob and she darted forward, nerves working a number on her. Awkward without her purse, which she normally dropped on the hall table, she pressed her hand to her face. She'd wanted this—wanted Caleb—for so long. Even when she'd denied wanting him, she realized now, she had, indeed, wanted him. She'd spent so much time feeling guilty for that desire, for driving him away, that this—here, now—felt somehow wrong. Like a bad deed that would be punished.

Shay swung around to face Caleb, finding him close—so tall and broad and gorgeous, she almost forgot what she'd intended to say. He reached for her. Somehow, she retained some logic and stepped backward. If he touched her, she'd forget everything but him. She'd forget that talk they'd never had. They had to have that talk. "What if we regret this?"

He laced the fingers of one of his hands with hers. "What if we don't?"

Fretful, she rejected that nonanswer. "What if we do, Caleb?"

"The only regret I'll have is walking away and losing another day pretending we don't want each other."

Sending him away would be hard. It would stink. But... "But what if something does go wrong? What if it makes you afraid to come around the family?" She frowned when she noticed he was smiling. "What about this is amusing?"

"The part where you still say 'what if' at the beginning of every sentence when you are feeling out of control," he admitted unashamedly.

"I'm serious, Caleb," she said, refusing to be drawn into playful banter designed to redirect her questions. "What if it's not what we thought it would be? Will we act strangely? All this build-up. What if—"

"What if—" he drew her wrist to his lips "—I kiss you here." His mouth pressed to her pulse point, and she felt it all over her body. "Or here?" He opened her palm and kissed it, as well. "Or even here?" He kissed the bend of her arm, which was really, really sexy, in a way she'd never imagined. No one had ever kissed her there. Shay shuddered with arousal.

His lips lifted with satisfaction as he asked, "At what point will I convince you...it's going to be good?" He folded her in his arms, his body cradling hers, his lips near her ear. "Because it's already good for me."

Shay buried her face in his neck, inhaling the scent of him. "I'm just—" she hesitated and decided to be honest—this was Caleb after all "—nervous." She laughed. "Yeah. I'm really nervous."

He pulled back, his hand sliding down her hair. "I'm still me," he said, his eyes warm with comfort. "The same guy you once pushed into the swimming pool, ruining my boots."

A sudden spell of laughter bubbled from her lips. She should have known he'd come up with the perfect thing to calm her nerves. "You were so mad. I'd venture to say you were furious."

"And you never told me why you did it," he reminded her.

"I don't remember," she said coyly, but of course, she did. She'd worn a dress to get his attention, and he'd told her it was too old for her, treated her like a kid sister. Not fifteen minutes later, she had the opportunity and took it. Caleb went into the pool, fully clothed. Seeing him sopping wet had done a lot to ease the bite of his reprimand.

"Liar," he purred, nibbling at her neck and picking her up, his hands sliding around her backside. Shay wrapped her legs around his waist, her arms wrapping around his neck. "Why'd you push me into that pool?"

"I was sixteen and hormonal, and you were in the way," she said, which was the truth—just not the whole truth. She intended to keep her youthful pettiness to herself.

Caleb headed down the stairs toward the living room, rather than toward the bedroom, and she knew it was because she'd told him she was nervous. The man was full of all kinds of awesomeness. Big, brawny and manly, yet he could be so darn sensitive.

"Liar," he accused, sitting down on the couch and taking her with him.

Shay automatically leaned into him, her hands leveraging her weight on his shoulders, the *V* of her body intimately spread across his cock. He was hard, his eyes hot, his hands gentle as they caressed her back. Thin layers of clothing separated them, but nothing more. Clothes that would soon be removed. And she knew he was thinking the same thing. She could see it in the heaviness of his eyelids, the tightness around his mouth.

"You were mad at me over the dress," he said softly, sliding his hands under her T-shirt, his calloused fingers brushing the skin of her midsection with delicious friction. "I wanted to turn you over my knee and spank you for strutting around half-naked, inviting that kind of attention. You were asking for trouble."

"Spank me?" she repeated. Something about her bare butt across his lap was so erotic. Maybe because she knew he would never really hurt her. But what he might do was please her, and that intrigued her. A slow smile slid onto her lips, and the familiar teasing between them banished her nerves. "Might have been fun."

He didn't laugh. Heat flared in his expression, arousal etched in his face. He molded her closer, pressing her body tight against his, bringing his lips a warm breath from hers. "Watch out," he warned softly, "or you might get more than you asked for."

Had any other man said that to her, she would have probably run for the hills. She certainly wouldn't have volleyed the seductive challenge back at him. But this was Caleb, and they not only volleyed, they volleyed well together. "Or maybe *you* will," she warned softly.

He studied her, his eyes hungry and a bit primal, before he smiled and nipped her lips with his teeth, soothing the bite with his tongue. "I thought you were nervous?"

"I changed my mind." Her fingers went to his face, her mouth to his, where she whispered, "I've wanted you too long to waste our time being nervous."

A low growl escaped his lips, the intensity matching that look he'd given her—masculine and rough, in a way that stroked a path down her nerve endings and right to her core. A second later, and not soon enough, Caleb's tongue parted her lips, tasting her with hot, wet demand. And she loved it—loved that after all those years of wanting him, of trying to push him over the edge, he was falling and taking her with him.

And finally, finally, he was touching her, and doing so with confidence and skill, without trepidation. He'd made up his mind this was happening. There was no turning back. *Thank God,* she thought. He touched her back, her hair and—*yes, please*—her breasts. Shay moaned into his mouth as he filled his palms and kneaded. Moaned again as his mouth traveled to her neck, her shoulder.

His fingers splayed wider on her bare skin and then began inching her shirt upward, pausing as his eyes found hers, searching, a silent question in the air—*do you want to stop?* She pressed her lips to his and let them linger, before murmuring, "I want you so very much, Caleb Martin." Shay leaned back and pulled her shirt over her head and tossed it aside, leaving her sexy Victoria's Secret pink bra in place, thankful now that she hadn't been able to find her plain T-shirt bra when she'd left this morning.

"You're beautiful," he said, his fingers trailing over the curve of one breast, a light, barely there touch with the effect of a mist over the ocean, splaying tingling eroticism through her entire body. His arm wrapped around her waist, and he lowered his head, mouth pressed hotly to the center of her chest. His hand and mouth traveling, mouth exploring the delicate line of her breastbone. Somehow he unhooked her bra without her knowing.

Shay caught it before it fell. Caleb arched a brow at her action, his hands stilling at her waist. "Second thoughts?"

It was her turn to give him a slow smile. She'd been teasing Caleb unmercifully for ten years—a dress here, a sexy top there. An accidental-on-purpose touch. Tonight somehow wouldn't be right if she broke her pattern.

"Why don't I show you how nervous I am?" she suggested. She pushed out of his lap and stood before him. Out of reach—that was key. He'd touch when she said he could touch. And she was planning on giving him a reason to want to touch. Shay let the bra drop to the ground.

10

CALEB DID NOTHING to disguise the raw hunger in his stare as his gaze raked over Shay's naked breasts, his body thrumming with demand. He wanted to take her, to rip her clothes off and find his way inside her, this woman who'd driven him to the brink so many times. That she was special, that she was undressing for him by choice, was as close to heaven on earth as he'd ever been. Or he was lying half-dead somewhere on a mission and hallucinating about Shay. It was one hell of a hallucination, at that.

Her breasts were high and full—he'd known that from her bikini and the many low-cut tops she'd intentionally worn for him. Tormenting him. She had absolutely, completely tormented him. But now, he had her, and he had an answer to a question he'd contemplated plenty of times over the years since that birthday kiss. Her nipples were not red and ripe, but pale rosy pink, as perfect as her ivory skin.

She kicked off her shoes, her pretty pink-painted toenails somehow a seduction of their own. Every little detail about Shay enticed him. And when she started to wiggle her jeans down her hips, her breasts wiggling with them, he had to force himself to rein in his control, to sit back against the couch cushion, loose-limbed. Otherwise, he would take the lead, he would take control. He wanted her too much not to. But he also wanted to know what she'd do next.

And he got his answer—and it wasn't what he expected—but then maybe it should have been. She discarded her jeans and before he could fully appreciate the neatly trimmed triangle of blond hair between her spectacular legs, she turned and sashayed toward the brown chair, her gorgeous backside on full display.

"Your turn," she said, sitting down in the chair and crossing her legs, as if intentionally blocking his view. Her hands dangled off the high arms of the chair, her eyes lit with challenge. "Undress for me, Caleb."

He sat there a minute and then laughed. Leave it to Shay to tempt, dare and tease. "And if I'd rather come over there and kiss every inch of your beautiful body?"

She lifted her chin and cast him a haunting look. "Then *I* might have to spank you."

His cock twitched. He was going to make Shay pay for her tormenting. "We'll see who's spanking who," he said, pushing to his feet. He stopped in front of her, tugged his shirt over his head and tossed it aside.

She sat up, hands by her sides, as if she intended to get up. He bent down and planted his hands on the sides of the chair. "Not so fast, Shay-Shay. I'm not done with you in the chair. You like playing with fire, don't you?"

"I like playing with you, but I'd like it better without your pants."

"If I get naked, I'm going to find my way inside you damn hard and fast," he assured her. "And I still have some playing of my own to do."

She inched forward in her chair, her breasts high, her nipples inviting, and reached for his pants. "I like hard and fast," she said breathlessly, her hand stroking his cock, tracing the ridge. "And I can tell that's exactly what you need." She pressed her lips to his abs and then surprised him by palming his crotch at the same time that her tongue dipped beneath his belt line, to where the head of his cock bulged. Her tongue lapped the head, to the liquid pooling on the tip. She eyed him and licked her lips. "You taste like you want hard and fast."

"Witch," he murmured, going down on the ground in front of her, his hands settling on her thighs. "I'm not done playing yet." He leaned down and kissed her knee, stroking her calf at the same time. "I want to know how you taste."

"Just like a man," she said. "Always have to be in control."

"I can assure you," he said, inching her legs apart, "if I had control, I'd have my pants off by now." She'd had him under her influence since the day he'd met her. He ran his hands up her inner thighs. "You're spectacular." His thumbs brushed the dampness clinging to her blond curls, his gaze taking in the pretty pale skin beneath it. She sucked in a breath at the touch. Whispered his name.

He leaned in as if he would taste her, letting his hot breath linger above the dampness of her arousal, but he didn't kiss her, didn't lick her. She moaned a plea.

He slid his hands upward over her waist as he admired her breasts, filling his hands and then using his fingers and his tongue to tease her nipples. Suckling and licking. She arched her back and moaned, her hands in his hair. She was so free with him, so willing to offer herself. And he knew she wasn't like this with everyone. Knew how prim and reserved she could be. His little she-wolf.

The thought drove him wild. He kissed her, twining his hands in her hair, suckling her tongue, nipping her lips. Hungry. So. Damn. Hungry. "Have I convinced you this is going to be good?"

She laughed, agreeing.

He smiled and untwined her arms from his neck. "Then you won't mind if I do this." He sat back on his haunches, gently tugged her forward, to the edge of the cushion. Then, his eyes pinned hers as he lifted one of her long sexy legs and drew her ankle to his lips. Her lips parted, her lashes fluttered.

Caleb licked, kissed and caressed a path up her leg before finding wet curls framing her swollen clit. He raised her other leg over his shoulder and then closed his mouth around her. She moaned and grabbed the arms of the chair, and he slid his fingers inside her. She arched into his mouth, into his touch, and he laved her with his tongue, unable to get enough of the sweet honey taste of her. Enough of her moans. She rocked desperately against his hand before spasming around his fingers, her body jerking with the intensity.

He tried to take her down slowly, to sensually tease her to final satisfaction, but the minute her spasms slowed, she lifted her head. "Now, please, will you take your pants off?"

***

BLESS BE, HE WAS FINALLY NAKED, because all Shay could think about right now was how much she needed to feel him next to her, in her. Feel him, yes. She needed him. The orgasm had shifted something inside her, triggered emotion, vulnerability.

He must have sensed the shift in her, because he'd barely given her a chance to admire his magnificent body, all roped muscle and defined masculine lines, before he lifted her from the chair and sat down in her place.

Shay straddled him, his thick—and impressive—shaft pressed to her backside. Instinctively, she reached behind her and touched it, stroked.

Intensity, desire, brutal handsomeness—all etched his face. And so did pain. He reached for her hand and settled it in front of him. "Condom. I forgot condoms." He squeezed his eyes shut as if he couldn't bear the thought of stopping.

She leaned forward, pressed her lips to his, then whispered, "I'm on the pill." She'd been engaged. She'd been sexually active. She'd never been sexually satisfied. Until tonight. His eyes lifted and she said, "Unless you're worried about—"

He pulled her forward, her chest to his, and kissed her, a deep, demanding kiss that tasted possessive and angry. It stole her breath, it tightened her chest. It turned her on. His fingers tangled in her hair, and with a gentleness that defied what she felt in his kiss, he eased her head back, pinned her in a dark stare. "You were on the pill for the guy you almost married," he said roughly.

His directness surprised her, but she'd never lied to Caleb, and she wasn't going to start now. "Yes."

"Did you love him?"

"No," she said without hesitation. "I should have. He was a good man. But I didn't."

He studied her a long moment, as if deciding whether he believed her. His mouth met hers, and she pressed her hand to his chest, when an uncomfortable thought occurred. He'd been out of reach, out of touch. "Were you ever...married?"

"Never even close," he told her.

They stared at one another, the air thick with implication. This time she let him kiss her. She had no idea where this was going, no idea why his answer had mattered so much, or why he'd cared about hers. A frenzied rush of kissing and touching. Of melding their bodies together, until he lifted her hips and guided her. Shay reached behind her and wrapped his shaft with her hand. It was hard and hot and pulsed in her hand. She gasped as she slid down him, felt him deep inside her. Caleb was inside her. They shared an intense look for several seconds before somehow, someway, they both ended up smiling.

Caleb's hands slid around her backside and leaned her forward, her mouth near his before he smacked her cheeks. Shay's breath caught in her throat at the erotically charged connection, her body clenching around his cock. Her eyes shutting. His fingers plucked at her nipples, rough and...exactly right. She'd never thought she liked rough. Not that, by any means, he was being too rough. No. He was exactly right.

Before she knew it, her nipple was in his mouth. Shay rocked her hips against his, the sway tugging the stiff peak, but he held on, suckling with delicious pressure, creating shock waves of pleasure to the center of her body. She wanted more. Of him. Of the sweet tug on her nipple. Reality slid away. There was only Caleb, and the ache to feel him deeper and harder. And this blissful sense of not thinking...not wondering what he was thinking. Knowing he wanted what she did on some level, that threw inhibition to the wind.

But the erotic tension, the sexual frenzy, shifted yet again. Shifted in the depths of a kiss. Turned to a slow seductive dance of their bodies that settled around them with the warmth of shared emotion. Soft touches, shared looks. Gentle, satisfying touches. Shay felt the edge of orgasm only seconds before it rushed over her. She moaned into Caleb's mouth and felt her breath catching in her throat. The first spasm jerked her body, the feel of him inside unbelievably good. She would have moaned if she'd been capable. Instead, she buried her face in Caleb's neck and clung as one ripple after another clamped down on his body and sent darts of pleasure all through her limbs. A low guttural sound slipped from Caleb as he pressed her hips down and thrust hard inside her. She felt the pulse of his release as his hand came to her head, and he leaned his face into her neck. Shay relaxed against Caleb. "Mmm," she murmured softly, utterly sated.

They didn't move for some time, holding each other, saying nothing, doing nothing, but just...being. A little piece of reality slid back into her mind and Shay swatted it away. But it came back, and she wondered if her silent satisfaction might be his silent guilt.

She pulled back to look at him, cupping his face in her hands. "Is this where we have an awkward 'after' moment? Whoops, we just had sex."

"After is a long time away, sweetheart," he said and pushed to his feet, her body still wrapped around his. "Where's the bedroom?"

11

SHAY WOKE ON HER STOMACH to the erotic touch of Caleb's hand on her backside. She sighed in contentment as his hand caressed her back, her shoulders. She blinked awake to find the room dark, but for a dim, shadow-inducing light coming from behind her, most likely from the bathroom.

"Do Aces not sleep?" she murmured without turning to face him, nestling down lower in the pillow. After hours of making love, she was both satisfied and bone tired. If he wanted her again, he'd have to work for it. And she wouldn't complain. He was pretty darn good when he wanted to be convincing. "The sun isn't up yet."

"I have a sunrise jump," he reminded her, his lips brushing her shoulder.

Shay shivered against the touch at the same instant that her stomach clenched. He was leaving. This was where that awkward moment happened. The goodbye and we'll talk. Later. Or maybe they wouldn't. This was that forbidden temptation satisfied. Only, she wasn't satisfied. Not even close. But now, she'd know if this were nothing but that for him. Now she'd have to move on. She inhaled. And she would. If this was a "bye, see ya" kind of thing to him, she'd move on. She'd finally move on. But it was going to hurt.

He smacked her on the backside playfully. "So get up, Shay-Shay. We have to leave in fifteen minutes."

"What?" she asked, rotating to her side to face him, resting her weight on her elbow. "I'm not going to jump out of a plane."

"I didn't think you were," he said, scooting close to her. His hand settled possessively on her hip. "You can sleep in my trailer while I jump."

"I...no. No, I'll stay here."

"Not a chance in hell," he said. "I'm not leaving you here and have you start wondering if I'm having regrets."

She wanted to deny she'd do such a thing, but instead asked, "Are you?"

"My only regret will be getting out of bed," he said. "But the very fact that you asked confirms it. I know you, Shay. You're already thinking too much about what I might be thinking, and fretting over the possibilities. If you're with me, and you want to know what I am thinking or feeling, then you can ask. Better yet, I'll tell you, so you don't have to ask. I don't want you conjuring it up in your head because I had to run off like this."

"I'll be asleep," she claimed, though it was doubtful. He was right. She'd be awake—fretting. "I won't have time to conjure anything."

He moved closer, his gaze flickering over her breasts for a hot instant. "If you come with me," he said, his fingers caressing her cheek, "I can finish my jump and then climb into bed with you and go back to sleep. We can wake up and do the morning after, the right way."

"Which is what?"

"Waking up next to each other, making love and then eating a big breakfast that all the lovemaking made a necessity."

Her chest tightened. "Caleb," she said softly, "what are we doing?"

"That's what we're figuring out, sweetheart," he said. "But so far, whatever it is, I like it."

She opened her mouth for a "what if," and he kissed her. "We're figuring it out, Shay. Once and for all, we're figuring it out."

Shay inhaled a hard-earned breath and nodded, but tension curled in her body, a warning they were treading on dangerous territory. But then he kissed her all over again, and the only thing she cared about was the next silky caress of his tongue. And the enticing idea of waking up next to him, in his bed.

***

CALEB FINISHED OFF the coffee he and Shay had grabbed on the road and reached across Shay's lap, where she sat next to him, to set his cup in the cup holder by the radio. "Two months out of the Army and I'm already soft," he said, his hand sliding to her leg. "I used to go days without sleep, but I'm feeling it now in a big ol' Texas-sized way." He realized what he'd said, and knowing Shay, he squeezed her leg and cast her a sideways look. "It was worth it." His gaze slid back to the road. "And I didn't feel the lack of sleep when I was in the Army because I was on an adrenaline rush called 'running for my life.'" He winked. "And I have you here, to suffer with me."

She gave a delicate snort. "I'm going to bed and not even superstrong coffee is keeping me up. I've never done well without sleep."

And he had every intention of taking her straight to his trailer and tucking her in bed—his bed. Granted there wasn't much in that trailer, but it was his, and he wanted her there. He'd made the decision to stop running from what was between them, and once he made a decision, he stood his ground. Yesterday proved to him that the only way he and Shay could hide what they felt from family and friends was to completely avoid each other—and they were too good together for him to want to.

Caleb turned down the dark dirt path leading to the Hotzone and had driven about half a mile to the gates when he spotted a vehicle on the left shoulder of the road.

He glanced at Shay. "This is private property, and I don't know that car. I better check it out." He stopped a couple of car lengths away from the vehicle and put the truck in Park. The absence of an obvious owner of the car set him on edge. Something was off here. "Remind me I need to make it a priority to put lights up along this path," he murmured, reaching across Shay to grab the gun he kept in the glove box, when she pointed out the window.

"Caleb. Look."

He sat up to find a petite female running toward the truck and waving her hands. "Help!"

Caleb grabbed his gun. "Stay here." He shoved it in his waistband.

"A gun, Caleb?" Shay gasped.

He didn't answer. He got out of the truck and headed toward the fortysomething woman. "What's happening, ma'am?"

The woman screamed something he didn't understand in Spanish and then said in English, "Help me." She heaved out a breath, a cell phone in her hand. "My husband...my husband. Can't..." She sobbed and dropped her phone. "Can't get it to work."

Caleb inched up on the woman, her face tear-streaked. "We get bad service out here." He kept his voice low and even. "I'll help you. Where's your husband?"

"Dead! He's not breathing. He's by the car." She fell to her knees and grabbed her phone. "Have to get help."

Behind him, the truck door opened. He knew Shay—she'd want to help the woman. At this point, for all Caleb knew, the woman had brought her husband out here and killed him, and was still armed with the weapon. Crazier things had happened. He wasn't letting Shay near her.

He held out his hand to Shay. "Not yet, Shay," he ordered.

"Caleb—" she started to object.

"Not until I know exactly what's going on," he said, without taking his eyes off the woman. He knelt beside her. "What happened to your husband?"

She sobbed. "He..."

Caleb touched her arm. "What happened?"

She inhaled and let it out. "He was changing the tire, and he just fell over." Her face crumbled. "He died." The last word was a shriek.

Shit. Shit. Shit. Caleb was on his feet, tossing his keys to the dirt in front of Shay, so they wouldn't accidentally hit her. "Drive ahead to the office and call 911 on the landline," he yelled. "There should be someone there, but if not, the red key is the one you'll need to get in."

She grabbed them up and started running to the driver's side of the truck. He faced the crying woman. "Keep trying 911," he ordered. She kept crying. More forcefully he yelled, "Dial the phone if you want to save your husband."

He didn't wait to see if she would reply. Seconds counted with a heart-attack victim, which was what he was betting this was. Caleb took off running toward the couple's car, dialing his phone at the same time, hoping his service would come through. It didn't. Damn. He rounded the car and just as the woman had said, her husband—as he assumed the man to be—lay on his back, by the tire he had been trying to change.

As a trained medic, Caleb's instincts kicked in and he went to work on the man. The man's wife appeared above him, whimpering and screaming erratically, but he tuned her out and focused on the life he was trying to save. Finally, finally, he found a light pulse and leaned back, hands on his pants.

Damn it, he needed an ambulance. He could only do so much, and he worried about brain damage. The guy had been without a pulse too long. He was contemplating driving the man to the hospital when sirens sounded in the distance.

"Good girl, Shay," he whispered, not at all surprised she'd come through.

Caleb pushed to his feet and ran toward the sound, to flag the ambulance and update the crew, when his cell phone rang on his belt. Of course. Now the tower worked. He snatched it up without looking at caller ID. "Stay where you are, Shay," he said. "I'll come to you."

"Shay?" Kent said. "What the heck is Shay doing with you at the crack of dawn?"

Caleb opened his mouth to say "Jumping out of a plane at sunrise," but it was too little, too late—the line was dead.

"Damn!" he said, punching the air. What was Kent doing calling him at this time of the morning? The ambulance screeched to a halt, and Caleb rushed to meet it. He had a life-or-death emergency to deal with before he took a beating from either Kent or Shay—or maybe both.

***

BY 9:00 A.M., SHAY HAD MET members of the San Marcus police, the fire department and the EMS crew, as well as both of Caleb's partners, Bobby and Ryan, and Ryan's new wife, Sabrina. To say her morning had been crazy was an understatement, and thanks to Sabrina, she now sat in the break area of the Hotzone, with the blissful high of freshly brewed coffee and a glazed donut.

"I can't believe Caleb took divers out to jump after everything that happened," Shay said, sipping her coffee.

Sabrina reached for a donut. Her third. Shay felt a hint of fan-girl admiration for the other woman, who could not only chow down on sweets and look slim and trim, but also wrote a syndicated political column that Shay admired.

"The Aces don't rattle easily," Sabrina said. "They were in a war zone most of the last decade. And though they can't talk about most of their missions, I know they were in dangerous territory, pretty much daily. What seems traumatic to us—" she raised her cup "—it's just spilled coffee to them."

Shay considered that statement. Caleb still felt like Caleb, but how could he be unchanged after living ten years under such intense pressure?

Sabrina continued, "They're cool under pressure, and it makes the customers feel comfortable. Heck, I was terrified to jump at first, but I jump now."

"Really?" Shay asked. "I'm not so keen on the idea."

"I'm still not a big fan of jumping, unlike Jennifer, who's an addict. But Ryan sweet-talks me past my nerves every now and then. So you've never jumped?"

"No," Shay said quickly. "And I don't plan on it, either. I'm taking flying lessons, though, and I'm enjoying it. I can deal with being in the driver's seat where I'm in control. The idea of jumping out of a plane and not being sure the chute will open...no, thank you."

Sabrina's eyes lit. "That's exactly how I feel." She sipped her coffee. "Flying lessons, huh? That sounds intriguing. Where do you do something like that?"

"A small airfield in Round Rock," she replied, and then without hesitation—Sabrina felt like one of those rare instant friends—she added, "You should come out and give it a whirl." There was a pad and paper on the table, and Shay wrote down her number. "Call me and we'll set it up."

"I might just do that," she said. "In fact, I probably will." She looked thoughtful. "I wish Jennifer was here to meet you. She's a vet and has a Sunday clinic. Although, you may be happy she's not here. She's always trying to fix Caleb up, afraid he feels out of place as the only single guy in the mix. I keep telling her she can't just marry him off. Oh, man. You better beware. She'll be planning your wedding before you know it. This may be worse than her attempts at blind dates on his behalf."

Wedding. Shay gulped. Her and Caleb? "Oh, no," Shay said, sitting up straighter. "We're not... I mean..." Her shoulders slumped. "It's complicated."

Sabrina set her elbows on the table. "Isn't it always?"

"My family raised him after his parents died," she said. "I'm sort of like, well, his sister."

"Oh," Sabrina said, her cheeks flushing. "I'm so sorry. I thought you were...seeing each other. I mean when I saw you together, there was a connection. I guess I misread it."

"You didn't," Shay said, hands wrapping around the coffee cup, her lashes lowering before lifting. "We've always battled an attraction. Now that he's home...we're trying to figure it out. But he and Kent, my brother, are close and—"

"Kent's your brother?"

Shay frowned. "Yes. You know him?"

"No," she said. "But he called three times this morning while I was answering the phone, trying to reach Caleb."

"Oh, God," Shay said, her heart kicking into a charge. "I don't have my phone. What if something is wrong? I should call." She started to get up and sat back down, queasy from worry and no sleep. "I can't call. He'll know I'm with Caleb at this early hour, and he'll ask why and..." She pressed her hand to her head. "This isn't going to work. My family is going to find out, and it's going to be a disaster."

Sabrina reached out and touched her arm. "Easy. I asked Kent if it was an emergency the last time he called, and he said no. He said Caleb knew what it was about."

Shay relaxed a little. "No emergency. Thank you. This whole thing has me a nervous wreck. I shouldn't be with Caleb, and I know it. I mean my family is his family. I can't jeopardize that for him, but I'm selfish I think. I can't seem to help myself. What does that say about me?"

"Shay," Sabrina said, "I hope you don't mind me saying this—I mean we just met—but...if you two have been pining for each other as long as it sounds like you have, across thousands of miles, how can you not explore what's between you? Just keep it your secret for now. Then there is no family damage if it doesn't work out." She smiled. "Though you'd better be careful you two don't 'vibe' too heavily as a couple in front of them. You two connect. It's obvious."

Which is what Caleb had said. They weren't hiding what was between them. The family would figure it out. And they had to go see them all today.

Sabrina added, "That's why I was confused when you first said you two were family."

Caleb's voice rumbled in the background, and Shay looked up to find him standing in the doorway, dressed in a green flight suit, his light brown hair wind-rumpled and sexy. "Ready to get some sleep?"

"Do we even have time?" she asked. "We have to be at my folks' in a few hours."

"We can snag an hour to keep us standing," he said. "It's better than nothing."

The receptionist yelled from behind Caleb. "Caleb—Kent's on the phone."

Caleb's expression didn't change—if he was affected by the call, he didn't show it. "I'll call him back," he called over his shoulder, and then added to Shay, "Let's go get some rest."

The receptionist called back. "He wants to talk to Shay."

Shay stood up. "Kent knows I'm here?"

"Tell him I'll get back to him," Caleb told the receptionist.

Sabrina pushed to her feet. "I'll leave you two to hash this out. Shay, I'll call you about the flying lessons." She quickly scooted out the door and Caleb let her.

"Caleb," Shay demanded.

"Let's go to the trailer and I'll explain."

"Explain now."

12

CALEB SHUT THE DOOR to the break room and recapped his call with Kent from earlier in the morning. And his plan to deal with Kent. "I'll tell him you came out for a sunrise jump. Just like he did."

"He's never going to believe that, Caleb," Shay said. "Kent knows me. He knows I won't skydive."

"We'll convince him."

She pressed her hands to her face. "This is a mess." Her hands fell away. "What were we thinking?"

Caleb stepped forward and settled his hands on her shoulders. "Shay, sweetheart, you're exhausted, and exhaustion has a way of making things look bigger than they are. We'll convince him. We can do it."

She rested her head on his chest and hugged him. "I am so very tired, Caleb."

"I know, baby," he said, sliding his hand down her hair, and thinking how wonderful she felt in his arms. He tilted her head up, framed her face. "I'll call Kent, and then we'll go get some rest. I'll convince him. He might know you, but I know him. Let's go to the trailer first, though, because once I tell him what went down out here this morning, he's going to talk my ear off. You can be resting."

"Why would he even call you so early?"

"Knowing Kent," he said, "he was up all night playing poker, and knew I had a morning jump, so he called to brag."

She sighed. "That sounds like Kent. But call him now. I need you to call him now."

One look at her determined stare and Caleb knew he wasn't waiting until he got to the trailer. He grabbed the phone on the wall. Kent answered in two rings.

"What the hell is going on?" Kent asked. "Shay's out there with you, and she's not answering her phone. You won't take my calls. Is there something you want to tell me, Caleb?"

Kent's hot attitude gave a glimpse of what the future might hold, because it was clear Kent believed he and Shay were involved and he wasn't happy. "Shay did something stupid and I promised I wouldn't tell you about it if she skydived. But since she chickened out, I'll tell you. She locked her keys in her car at her office. Which, of course, with that fancy car of hers, means I have to take her to the dealership to get another key later today. Though I hear you're responsible for losing her spare keys."

Shay smiled, because she knew that last part about Kent losing her spare keys would ring true and add validity to her excuse for being with Caleb. When all was said and done, Kent had confirmed that, yes, he'd been up playing poker all night and so had Shay's parents, and her father had won big. He'd be taking Shay's mother shopping on Kent's dime. And now, to Shay's utter dismay, Shay could tell that Kent had just asked to borrow money from Caleb.

When he finally hung up, Shay said, "I can't believe he just did that." She pressed her lips together and dared to say what she'd been thinking for a while now. "I think he has a gambling problem. He can't even control himself in his own family environment."

"Your dad probably thought Kent lost on purpose," he said. "To give him money for the trip."

"He makes a lot of money as a sales rep," she said, "but he has no savings. Not a dime. I'm worried."

Caleb drew her hand in his and pulled her to her feet. "I'll talk to Kent about it," he promised.

"Thank you," she said. "I've tried, but he won't listen to me. He respects you. I think you might be able to get through to him."

Caleb had a feeling he'd better have that talk before Kent found out about Shay and him, but he left that part out. "I'll do my best," he said. "But right now...I want you...in my bed. I've been thinking about it all morning."

"To sleep," she said playfully.

"Of course," he replied innocently.

A few minutes later, they walked hand in hand across the grassy back field between the office and his trailer. "It's nothing fancy, like your place."

"My house isn't fancy," she argued.

"I like your place," he said. "It looks like you, and it smells like you. And I happen to love how you smell." He kissed her hand. "My trailer, on the other hand, is a hole in the wall that came furnished from the prior Hotzone owners. I haven't bothered to do anything with it, because, once the Hotzone is past the new-business bumps, I plan to get something else. But I've spent more time in this hole the past two months than I've spent in one place in ten years. That makes it a castle." He paused at his door and pulled it open, before waving her forward. "So welcome to my castle."

Shay walked up the stairs and entered. Caleb shut the door and locked it, thinking they'd had enough surprises for one day. He turned to find Shay standing at the bar that separated the living area from a compact kitchen, holding a photo he had displayed of him and six other Aces in front of a plane.

He walked up beside her, and she glanced up at him. "Tell me about the man in this photo," she said, looking up at him. "Which one?"

"You," she said. "I want to know about you. About the man you were then."

"I was the same man I am now."

"I want to know who that is," she said, "because I know you saw things and did things. Hard, horrible things that have to haunt you. Yet you stayed ten years."

How did he explain the switch he could turn on and off, that allowed him to become a soldier separate from the man? The switch that kept him sane. "Most of my missions were top secret," he said. "I can't talk about them. But even if I could tell you, you don't want to hear about it, any more than I would want to remember."

"Then why keep doing it for ten years?"

"Someone has to do the ugly stuff," he said.

"But everyone doesn't decide it has to be them."

"I'm not the kind of guy who can go to work and pretend there aren't horrors worse than you ever imagined in this world," he said. "I'm the guy who makes sure others can just pretend."

She set the picture down. "I see." She turned away.

"Wow, sweetheart," he said, snagging her arm and turning her to face him. "What just happened?"

"Just promise me when you leave this time, you'll say goodbye, Caleb," she said, her voice shaking. "Because not saying goodbye—that was just not right. It hurt. And so did ten years of shutting me out. Don't do it again."

He pulled her close, stroked her hair away from her face. "Shay. I'm not going anywhere. I told you. I'm here to stay."

"No," she said. "You say that, but you'll never be satisfied taking amateur jumpers out for entertainment, Caleb. I saw you today. Saving lives is natural to you. You're one of the good guys, that's clear. That's something to be proud of. And I am. But you said so yourself—you didn't really want to leave the Army. This life will get old, lack purpose, and you'll reenlist."

He tried not to smile because her reaction wasn't just about being tired. She cared about him. Maybe she loved him. He was pretty damn sure he'd always loved her. "Were you aware, my little Shay, that the Hotzone is contracted to train a group of Special Ops candidates once a month? That I am, indeed, still very much involved with the Army?"

She blinked. "You are?"

"That's right," he said, and picked her up. "I don't have to go anywhere but here to make a difference." He carried her past the worn leather couch and chair, down the short hallway to the bedroom—just big enough for a bed and nothing else—and laid her down. He went down on the mattress. "Sleep. You're going to be nervous enough facing your family. Some rest will help." He brushed his lips over her forehead. "Unlike you, I never showered this morning. I'm going to take a quick one and I'll join you."

She sat up. "Don't go. Shower before we leave."

"If I don't go shower now," he said and winked, "you won't get any sleep."

***

SHAY HAD JUST HEARD the shower turn on when the sound of Caleb's cell phone ringing from the living room caught her attention. She slid off the bed and rushed down the hall, afraid it might be her service, or George, calling.

She found the phone lying on the counter by the photo she'd been looking at, and quickly checked caller ID, hitting Answer when she recognized the number. "George? Are you okay? I've been worried sick." The man was predictable to the second, and he'd been off radar fifteen plus hours. "You didn't show up for your appointment. I spent last night, and this morning, worrying something had happened to you."

"Sorry about that, Doc. Something urgent came up, as in I fell in love. I met someone. I haven't been so happy in years."

A red light flashed in her mind. "You suddenly fell in love and that made you miss an emergency appointment?"

"We'd had a fight," he said. "But she showed up at my house and all is well. I can't wait to tell you all about her when I get back from Mexico."

"Mexico?!" she sputtered. The man barely ever left his house. "You're going to Mexico?"

"Yes," he said. "And they just called our boarding group. I'll call you when I get home. Thanks for everything, Doc. I remember all those times you told me, loving someone means you could lose them, but it's better than never knowing them." He hung up.

Shay set the phone down and rushed to the bathroom to tell Caleb about George. He'd left the door open and she could hear the shower running. "My client called," Shay said, sitting down on the lid of the toilet.

He looked around the shower curtain. "And?"

"He said he met a woman and he's really happy."

He snorted. "He stood you up for a woman. Nothing we didn't know. Typical man. Always thinking with the wrong head."

"Coming from a man," she said.

He grinned. "I'm a soldier," he said. "Respect comes before all base needs." He disappeared behind the curtain.

She opened her mouth to crack a joke, but stopped. This wasn't typical behavior for George. And that fancy house of his screamed some sort of money source. That would make him a target for the wrong woman. Shay thought of George's pain over the loss of his wife. She thought of her fears that she and Caleb couldn't and shouldn't be together. That their family situation would end their relationship before it really got started, that he'd leave again, no matter how much he said he wouldn't. The truth was, the only thing for certain was the moment.

She eyed the curtain, his naked silhouette behind the semitransparent material. She might not ever get the chance to make love to Caleb in the shower ever again. Shay stood up and undressed.

Before she could talk herself out of it, Shay pulled back the curtain and stepped inside. The minute she took in the sight of his sinewy muscles dripping wet, Shay was glad she did.

"You do know this isn't the way to get any sleep," Caleb said softly.

"I can't sleep when you're wet and naked," she replied, letting him pull her close.

He smiled and moved so that his back took the brunt of the water, and she felt his erection press against her hip. "I'd be disappointed if you could."

She reached down and stroked his shaft, already impressively ready for her. "There's something I've always wanted to do to you," she confessed.

"There's a lot of things I've always wanted to do to you," he said. "I'd offer a demonstration, but it's going to take a whole lot longer than we have today."

"I'd rather focus on my 'to do to Caleb' list," she said, smiling. She kissed his chest and then slid down his body until she'd wrapped his cock in her hand and looked up at him. "If that's okay with you?"

"I'd say that ranks as not 'yes,' but 'hell, yes,'" he said, his hand settling on the wall, as if he suddenly needed support.

Shay smiled and ran her tongue along the base of his erection. "Oh, yeah," he said. "Definitely a 'hell, yes.'"

Hearing the gruff, aroused tone of his voice, Shay felt herself respond. Felt the ache between her thighs, the pinch of her nipples, the need to take him in her mouth. She enjoyed control, she knew she did. To control a man like Caleb, as powerfully hot as he was—that was as big a rush as she could imagine. Aside from maybe him controlling her, as contradictory as that might seem.

She lapped at the head and twirled her tongue around the ridge. He moaned and she sucked a few inches into her mouth, then a few more, slowly, deeply. Caleb's hand came down on her head, and Shay reveled in the thrust of his hips. In the proof that she was driving him to the edge, pleasuring him. She caressed his powerful legs, the flex of his nice tight backside, could feel his balls tighten, feel the desperation in his thrusts. Taste the salty promise that she would soon bring him to satisfaction, when he murmured her name, and pulled back.

She opened her mouth to ask him why he'd stopped her, but he lifted her to her feet and kissed her. He tasted of a man on the edge—of wild, untamed passion. Of desire barely contained. And she knew what it had cost him, not to let her finish him.

He pressed her against the wall, his hand sliding up her body, over her breast. Water, no longer hot, but warm, sprayed over their bodies, as he lifted her leg and pressed inside her, thrusting hard and deep.

Shay gasped as pleasure flooded her senses, and she clung to him, finding herself pinned in his hot stare as he said, "We're going to come together, just like we're going to face the family together this afternoon." He thrust again, stroking her into a whimper, before he demanded agreement. "Okay?"

"Yes," she said. "Yes, okay. Together." And before she could start thinking about what might go wrong with that plan, he took her away, to a place where together felt really good and sleep didn't matter.

13

CALEB PARKED HIS TRUCK in front of Shay's parents' place with Shay sitting uncomfortably on the opposite side of the truck, instead of by his side. He'd made her ride by his side until a few blocks away, not ready to play this game of not being together. But he didn't have a choice, and he knew that.

He wanted it over. And he wanted this to be it—the last time. By the time Shay's parents were back from Italy, he wanted their relationship to be public, and he intended to do everything he could to convince Shay of the same. If—and it was a big "if" as far as he was concerned—they decided this relationship didn't work, then at least they could stop dancing around each other. Either way, they would have resolution.

"I feel like they're going to know," Shay admitted, as he killed the engine.

"If they didn't know yesterday, when we were about to explode with sexual tension, they won't know today," he said, and then pointed. Her mother was coming out the front door directing her father, as he rolled a bag toward Kent's truck. "They're excited and nervous. They aren't going to be paying us any attention." He discreetly reached across the seat and squeezed her hand. "Let's get this behind us."

She nodded, drew a deep breath and exhaled before reaching for her door handle. Shay immediately rushed toward her parents, and he tried not to notice the way the light denim of her jeans hugged the sweet curve of her backside, the same one his hand had hugged less than an hour before. The slight expansion around his zipper region had Caleb slowing his pace, in no rush to join the chaos of pretravel jitters.

Kent shoved the screen door open and sauntered in Caleb's direction, trying to act nonchalant, but the stiff set of his jaw said he was far from relaxed. Kent's early obsessions with the racetrack had apparently been foreshadowing the future, a fear Caleb had begun to nurse on a visit several years back. This wasn't the first time Kent had asked him for money, and he still hadn't seen the return of the first loan. Not that he was biting at the bit to get it back. He had money. He was more concerned over the fact that Kent didn't have the money to return, and what that said about their suspicions of a gambling problem.

Kent stopped beside him, placing his back to the family. "Mom's making Dad crazy, she's so afraid of forgetting something," he laughed, but the sound was strained.

"They'll be fine once they get on the plane," Caleb said, and motioned to the house. "Let's go inside."

Kent nodded, and they walked in silence until they stood in the kitchen. Caleb tossed an envelope of cash on the island counter and then leaned on the counter, hands behind him. Kent snatched it up and stuffed it in his pocket, as if he feared it would be seen.

"Thanks, man," he said. "I know I owe you, and I'll pay you back. I have a bonus coming at the end of the year."

Caleb noted the smudges under Kent's eyes, the jerkiness of his movements. "You got the gambling bug pretty bad, don't you?"

Kent shoved his hands in his pockets and laughed. "I was gambling with Dad, Caleb."

"Last night," he said. "And still you lost your backside instead of walking away."

"It was Dad! He egged me on, and I didn't want to say no."

"You got a bookie?"

"Caleb, man," he said.

"Do you have a bookie, Kent?"

"I'm a single guy with no responsibility."

"So, you do."

Kent scrubbed his jaw. "I don't have a problem if that's what you're getting at."

"You don't have a dime to your name, Kent."

"I'm in a slump," he said. "My end-of-the-year bonus will fix that."

"Gambling's like drinking," Caleb said. "It's addictive. If you need help—"

"I don't," Kent said sharply, his voice lifting. He shook his head and lowered his voice. "Look, Caleb. I appreciate the help and the concern, but I'm fine. And I'll get this favor returned."

"I still can't believe I'm going to Italy," Sharon exclaimed as she rushed into the room. "Italy!" She hugged Caleb. "I love you, son, and not because of Italy. Because you're you." She patted his cheeks. "And you're so darn handsome." Before he could respond, she'd let him go and was talking. "I looked up the hotel online, and they have cooking classes. I'm going to come back and cook you all kinds of wonderful meals."

Caleb's gaze lifted to Shay, where she now stood in the kitchen doorway, looking awkward and downright upset. He patted his stomach. "I can't wait."

"Please tell me we're ready to leave," Bob grumbled as he slid into the doorway next to Shay. "If I don't get your mother on the plane with a glass of wine in her hand soon, I'm going to blow my top." He eyed Shay. "What's this about you locking your keys in your car?"

Shay glared at Kent. "You blabbed that fast."

"Didn't I?" Kent asked with a grin.

"That patient of yours must have had you flustered," her father added. "You normally don't do things like that."

"I was flustered," she agreed. "At Caleb acting like a bodyguard I didn't need."

"Oh, now," Caleb said, "that's where I have to object. Your building was dark and deserted. You shouldn't have been there alone."

"I've done just fine on my own for the last ten years, Caleb," she countered, clearly trying to maintain their normal siblinglike banter. "You've been home two months, and I've barely seen you, but suddenly, you're all over me and my business."

Caleb arched a brow, barely containing a laugh, because she was right. He was all over her and liking every minute. Shay's eyes registered what she'd said, and she paled.

"You're too independent sometimes," Bob said. "I'm glad Caleb is here to look after you while we're gone."

Shay crossed her arms in front of her body. "Oh, good grief," she said. "You'd think I wasn't a grown woman with a medical practice."

"The great thing about family," Bob said, "is no matter how grown up you are, you still get love and protection. And a good kick in the ass when you need it. And for the record, daughter of mine, going to an office building alone, in the dark, deserves a kick in the ass." He grabbed her and kissed her cheek, then eyed his wife. "Come, woman. We have a flight to catch.

Kent—chauffeur and baggage handler—get that bag by the door and take it to the truck."

Fifteen minutes later, Kent was off on his business trip and her parents were off on their adventure. Shay fell against the door after watching Kent's truck pull out of the driveway, packed with baggage and family, leaving Caleb and Shay alone. "Oh, my God, Caleb. I practically announced we were sleeping together when I said you've been all over me and my business." She hit her forehead. "What was I thinking?"

He chuckled and pressed a hand on the wall over her head. "No one caught that but me, but I admit, I almost laughed out loud."

"I know!" she said. "I saw your face and wanted to strangle you." She shook her head. "And Mom called you 'son.' *Son,* Caleb." She leaned her head against the door. "This, after we just had sex in your shower together. We're playing with fire here. They are never going to trust you again if they find out you're sleeping with me."

He smiled with the memory of that time in the shower—straddling her hips with his, his hand on her slender waist. "We had *amazing* sex in my shower."

"Exactly," she agreed as if that was the point. "Amazing sex makes it worse."

He wasn't even going to try and understand her logic, because there was none. "We're alone for two weeks, Shay. What would have seemed a nearly impossible feat, but we've achieved it. Let's just relax and enjoy being together."

She pressed her hands to his chest. "How do I relax when we're headed toward a crash-and-burn? I don't want you ostracized from the family, Caleb. They trust you to look out for me."

"I'm not breaking that trust, Shay," he said. "You need to know right now—I have no intention of keeping our relationship a secret. Not if we decide that's what this is. Either we're working through a fantasy or we're working toward a future. And I can tell you right now...I like who we are together. I like us, Shay. I don't want to throw that away because we're afraid of the family's initial shock that we're together."

She softened instantly. "I like us, too."

He slid his fingers under her hair, caressing the delicate skin of her neck. "Then let's be 'us' during this rare solitary time we have, and see where it leads. Don't think about what everyone else will say. Just you and me. Can you do that?"

Her lips trembled. "Yes. Yes, I'd like that."

He smiled. "Good." He kissed her temple, and then her jaw, and then her neck. "You smell like sunshine."

"I smell like your cologne," she said, a smile in her voice. "I was afraid someone would notice."

He pulled back and looked at her. "I'm really going to have to work on your paranoia," he said, his hands sliding up her sides, over her breasts.

She moaned. "Not here, Caleb."

"Oh, yes," he said. "Most definitely here." He shoved her T-shirt up and pressed down her bra, thumbing her nipples. "I've fantasized about you in this house too many times to miss this opportunity."

Her hands went to his arms, but she didn't push him away. "I have to get the key to my car before the car dealership closes," she panted.

"I'm staying the night at your place," he said. "I'll take you to work tomorrow and get the key before you leave work." His hand slid around her backside, and molded her to his hips, nuzzling his erection in the *V* of her body. "Problem solved."

"I don't remember inviting you to stay the night," she said.

"Oh, I remember," he said, brushing his lips over hers. "In the shower."

"I was being blackmailed at the time, if I remember correctly," she said. "You were withholding on me."

She'd wanted to come. He'd wanted assurance he could wake up to another shower adventure the next morning. "I'm staying the night tonight. And tomorrow night." He stared down at her. "And every night for at least the next two weeks."

She wet her lips. "At the end of the two weeks, Caleb, then what?"

"I'm sure we can come up with any number of possibilities. Right now. I'm trying to figure out which fantasy to act out first." He slid down to his knees in front of her. "The one where I strip you naked in the hallway seems a good place to start."

***

THE FOLLOWING FRIDAY NIGHT, almost a week into Shay and Caleb's little escape from the family, they sat in the corner of a dimly lit fondue restaurant with Jennifer, Sabrina, Bobby and Ryan. Dinner was over, and the women had gathered at one end of the table to talk while the guys did the same at the other end. Shay couldn't help but steal looks at Caleb here and there. The week had been such a wonderful whirlwind of all kinds of intimacy and pleasure. They'd spent the week at her place, but they planned to spend the weekend at his to accommodate his sunrise jumps.

Sabrina's phone rang, and she eyed the number and rolled her eyes. She looked at Ryan, who was tall and dark compared to Bobby's tall and blond, and held up the phone. "One guess."

"Your father," Ryan said, understanding immediately.

She nodded.

Ryan flagged the waitress and pointed to his wife. "We need another margarita right here."

Sabrina smiled and turned back to Shay and Jennifer. "Oh, I love that man. He knows exactly what I need. I should probably hire you to examine my head, Shay. I mean, my father is a politician. I write a political column. I know what happens when I disagree with one of his positions—I get the press, and him, on my backside. But what do I do? I write what I feel."

The waiter set a margarita in front of her, and she took a big drink.

"You might as well get used to this," Jennifer said, blowing blond hair from her eyes and reaching for Sabrina's drink to have a sip. "Every time she does this, we all need a drink."

Shay glanced at Caleb, who was watching her, a smile in his eyes, clearly enjoying having her here, in the midst of his friends. Shay liked it, too.

"So what do you say, Shay?" Sabrina asked. "Will you take me on as a patient?"

Shay laughed. "Not a chance," she said. "I never take on family or friends as patients. But off the record, my opinion is, it takes a confident, well-adjusted person to stand up for their own beliefs when you know you will feel some pain for doing so."

"Wow," Sabrina said. "You're good. That was the perfect thing to say."

Shay laughed. "If only my real patients were that easy." She glanced at Jennifer. "Sabrina's coming out to my flight lesson tomorrow. You should come."

"I wish I could," Jennifer said. "I have a clinic. My animals need me. But I'm loving the idea of the women of the Hotzone having their own wings. That's so cool. We'll show these guys they aren't the only ones with skill."

"It would be cool," Shay said, swallowing hard at the implications that she was already one of those Hotzone women. Fear gripped her throat. Fear this was too good to be true. Illogical fear she'd normally quickly decipher like a puzzle in a patient, but in herself, it was a struggle to understand. Her gaze radiated toward Caleb as it had so many times already. He was laughing at something Ryan had said, looking sexy and calm, and just watching him made her stomach flutter. She loved him. She loved him so much. More of that fear tightened in her chest.

Shay shifted her gaze from Caleb and set her napkin on the table. "I'm going to run to the ladies' room." She pushed to her feet and headed down toward the back corner of the restaurant.

The hallway was dark and vacant, and Shay pushed through into the single-stall restroom to find it empty. She'd barely shut the door when a knock sounded.

"Shay." It was Caleb.

Part of her yearned for a few minutes to think, but a bigger part reveled in him following, in how he always knew something was wrong or right. Shay opened the door.

Instantly, his hands settled on her waist, and he walked her back into the restroom and shut the door. "What upset you?"

Shay's eyes tingled—heck, her skin tingled—with the emotion that overcame her. "I knew you knew I was upset."

His hand stroked her hair. "Talk to me, Shay."

"I think I'm just overwhelmed," she said, being as honest as she could be. "A week ago I couldn't kiss you.

Now, I have Jennifer and Sabrina referring to me as one of the Hotzone women."

"Hotzone women," he repeated and smiled. "I like it."

She pushed away from him. "Caleb," she continued, "don't you see? I shouldn't be here, involved with your friends, until we know I'm staying involved. I think I'm liking this too much. I'm confused. I want—"

He tugged her close. "What do you want, Shay? Because I want you involved in every aspect of my life. There's no 'maybe' about it. A week isn't going to change that for me, and it's not going to change it for you."

"Caleb," she whispered, all that emotion welling in her chest, now stealing her voice.

"That's not the response I'm looking for," he said. "This is where you say you feel the same way."

"It's complicated, Caleb."

"It's not complicated for me. Either you want to be a part of my life, or you don't."

"So that's it?" she asked. "If I'm not a Hotzone woman, I'm not in your life at all? What about the rest of the family?"

He stared down at her for several tension-laden seconds. His hands dropped from her sides. "Is that what you want?" he asked, ice touching his voice. "To go back to the past?" A knock sounded on the door. "Go away," Caleb said stonily and then to Shay, he repeated, "Is that what you want?"

Panic flooded her at the realization she'd pushed him away, and she hugged him with all her might. "No. No. It's not what I want." She was barely holding back tears. She never cried. Shay looked up at him. He wasn't touching her. He was just letting her hold him. "I don't know what's wrong with me. I'm freaked out.

Scared. I don't know why, Caleb. I don't. This week has been one of the best of my life. I want this. I want you. I...I love you."

The magic words. He kissed her, those strong wonderful arms surrounding her, holding her close. And when he finally came up for air, he said, "Let's get out of here."

Before she could digest the words, he was opening the door and pulling her with him. They were back at the table in a flash, and Shay grabbed her purse, as Caleb said, "We're calling it a night."

"Meet you at the Hotzone tomorrow," Shay called to Sabrina, surprised to see her holding back a smile. As if they'd all expected the fast departure.

He led her to the truck, to the driver's side, and kissed her, a deep, searing kiss that stole her breath, before he opened the door and helped her in. Inside the truck he kept her close, searing her with a look, as he had with the kiss, and then he silently put the truck in gear. And Shay tried to cling to that kiss, to the look in his eyes, the look that said she was his world. Not to the silence that taunted her, that he had yet to tell her he loved her, too.

Suddenly, she was scared again—that he might actually love her back. She didn't know if she was ready to embrace the "coming out" to the family that might require. No. Not might. Would require. And then there was the fear that sex was all there really was between them—the possibility that their attraction was simply a long-burning fire that needed to be fully stoked before it could be extinguished. This could all be one big mistake, a giant bag of chocolate calling her name, promising big hips and lots of hours in the gym—however, resisting the bittersweet seduction was impossible. Not when Caleb had his hand on her leg, pushing her to the edge.

14

THE INSTANT THEY WERE inside the trailer, Shay found herself against the trailer door, Caleb pressed against her, kissing her. She forgot confessions of love. All she cared about was right here, right now. How much she needed him. And he needed her. Even if he didn't love her, she felt the raw greediness in him, the must-have, must-touch madness eating him alive, as it was her. It was enough. *For now,* she repeated in her head. For now.

In a frenzied rush, they began stripping away the layers of clothes. The first skin-to-skin connection jolted Shay's senses. He was so warm and hard all over. Her hands and body skimmed taut muscle. He was beautiful. Amazing.

Once their clothes were tossed here and there, and they were naked, Caleb's forehead rested on hers, his hands gently gliding down her shoulders, leaving goose bumps in their path. "You're amazing," he whispered.

She smiled. "I was just thinking the same thing about you."

"Were you?"

"Yes," she said, her fingers splaying over his chest, lingering on his nipples. "Oh, yes. You are most definitely the most amazing man I've ever known...seen."

With a low rumble in his throat, his hands cupped her backside, and he lifted her. Shay folded herself around him willingly, eagerly. She wrapped her arms around his neck, her legs around his waist, and clung to him, nipping his shoulder and his neck, while he headed toward the bedroom.

He went down on the bed on top of her, the heavy weight of him surrounding her, consuming her. Exactly what she needed. Shay breathed him in, willed him to take control. She didn't want control—not tonight. She wanted to forget. She wanted to feel. She wanted Caleb. On top of her, inside her. She inhaled his scent, drew him in.

He slid between her thighs, thick, pulsing. The promise of escape and pleasure. Her lashes fluttered shut, her hips arching as he used his cock to tease the sensitive folds of her body.

"Look at me," Caleb asked her gently, his fingers caressing her cheeks, her face.

Shay opened her eyes, and she wondered if she'd imagined the rigid mask he'd worn in that restroom, because the intense emotion in his face captured her soul.

He entered her then, pinning her in an emotion-laden stare, daring her to look away. But she didn't want to look away. Not even when he sank deep into the depths of her, stretching her, claiming her, the pleasure causing her to quiver. She clung to the emotion in his face, to the message there that said more than words ever could. She didn't want this to end. She wanted time to stop. He rotated his hips, deepened his position, settled on his elbows above her, lingering, savoring...unmoving. This is what she needed. *For now,* a voice whispered in her head, not letting her forget there would be a *later*.

Shay reached up and stroked the lines of his handsome face, traced his lip. He nibbled her fingers, slowly, sensually. She shoved the voice in her head aside and reached for his mouth, but he didn't give it to her. Instead, he slid his hands to her hair again—she loved the way he was always touching her hair.

"I had it all planned, you know? Telling the truth. The big confession. It would be just like now. Me inside you. Us together like one. So when it came in the bathroom of a restaurant, I couldn't bring myself to let go of the plan. To let it be less than how I'd planned it. The moment—this moment—when I would tell you, when I am telling you, that I can't stand the idea of living another day without you. I love you, Shay White. You are, without a doubt, everything that has been missing the past ten years, and I felt every last second of your absence."

Shay could barely breathe. "You love me."

A tender smile touched his lips. "Very much. Shay, I want to tell the family. I want to stop hiding. I want us to be together. We'll talk about how and when, but we have to do it."

"Yes," she agreed. "Yes."

He kissed her then, and Shay lost track of time, in the many ways they pleasured each other. In the number of times they said they loved each other. Shay fell asleep in his arms, in a happy bubble so wonderful, she didn't think it could ever burst.

That was until someone started pounding on the front door, jerking her to a sitting position, with Caleb following her. He glanced at the clock. "Who the hell is here at two in the morning?" He climbed over Shay to look out the window and cursed. "It's Kent."

"Kent?" Shay exclaimed.

"Yes," Caleb said, already standing up. "I guess we know he's home from his business trip." He scavenged for his pants and cursed. "My clothes are in the living room."

"Oh, God, so are mine," Shay said, her heart in her throat. "And my purse. You have to hide them. Hide anything that looks like me."

He stood there, naked, hands on his hips, and stared at her. "I thought we were done hiding."

"We are," she said. When the time was right. When she was sure nothing would go wrong. She had to try to make him understand. How could he not understand? "Having Kent find me in your bed when he's obviously here for some abnormal reason isn't likely to make him accept us as a couple, Caleb. We have to tell everyone the right way." A bad thought hit her. "What if he knows? What if he's here to confront you? What if he's going to pick a fight? What if—"

He cut her off. "He doesn't know, Shay." He shook his head. "Before I go see what he wants, let's be clear. You actually want to hide in the bedroom while I talk to your brother?"

"Yes," she said. "I have to."

He stared at her for a few hard seconds, during which more knocking ensued, and then said, "Whatever, Shay," and turned away, heading, in all his naked glory, toward the living room.

Oh, yeah. The happy bubble had definitely burst. He was unreasonable and mad.

***

CALEB STALKED TO the living room and shoved on his pants. He snatched up Shay's things and shoved them under a kitchen counter. It wasn't that she didn't want to tell her brother about them now. It was the something he saw in her eyes that was upsetting him. The panic. The certainty that she was nowhere near ready to come clean with the family about their relationship.

Again stalking, he headed to the door and yanked it open, to find Kent sitting on the front steps, his back to the door. Caleb flipped on the light and stepped outside, into the muggy night air. Kent didn't turn around, and that spoke volumes. He was having trouble facing Caleb.

Caleb scrubbed the stubble grazing his jaw and sat down next to him. Silent. He was there when Kent was ready to tell him why he was here.

"I screwed up, Caleb," Kent said. "I screwed up bad."

"You're here in one piece," he said. "Everything else is fixable."

He grunted and turned to lean against the wooden staircase, moonlight illuminating the sharp lines and strain of his face. "I was thinking about what you said about me not having a dime to my name. You were right. I'm pathetic."

Caleb turned to rest against the opposite railing. "I never said you were pathetic."

"You didn't have to," he said. "I'm saying it. I'm pathetic."

"You said you have a bonus coming," Caleb reminded him. "Use that to start saving, maybe make a safe investment. I can hook you up with the guy who has been managing my money while I was in the Army. I trusted him enough to give him say-so over my money when I wasn't capable of looking after it myself. It was his smarts, not mine, that put money in my bank account."

Kent leaned his head on the rail, and covered his face with his hand. "I screwed up, Caleb," he repeated. "I screwed up so bad."

"Maybe you better be specific," Caleb said. "What exactly did you do to screw up?"

He swallowed hard and dropped his hand. "I thought I needed to do something to get things right. One last bet. Get some money in the bank and then walk away. Cut the gambling thing altogether. I had a tip on a sure-thing horse, but I needed to bet big to make this the last time, to make it count."

Caleb went still. "You used a bookie and lost."

He nodded. "Yeah. I lost. And now, if I don't pay up, they'll pretty much break every bone in my body."

Caleb knew. He'd seen an Army buddy get devoured by a gambling habit. Even for someone well trained, a half-dozen baseball bats can do a hell of a lot of damage to an unarmed man. He'd survived because he had enough training to get out alive, and the Army had intervened and straightened his ass out. But not before his brake lines had been cut, and he'd crashed into a tree to avoid another car.

"How much?"

Kent's head fell back against the wall. "I bet my entire bonus, like an advance on the money I knew I had coming. It seemed a perfect plan. I thought I could pay you back and get money in the bank and—"

"How much, Kent," Caleb said sharply.

"Twenty," he said, and looked at Caleb. "Twenty thousand."

Caleb cursed. "Twenty thousand dollars? Are you flipping nuts?"

"Caleb, I thought—"

"Don't, Kent. Don't tell me you thought, you planned, you knew. Because you didn't. You're right. You screwed up." He stood up and paced the porch, pacing off anger, before he stopped. "I'll give you the damn money, but you *are* paying me back."

"Of course," Kent said. "I'll write you a post-dated check for bonus time. I swear, Caleb, my bonus covers this. I swear. I know I screwed up. I know."

"You're damn right you're paying me back every dime, and you know how I know? Because it's coming with conditions. Like help. And not help you tell me you're going to get. Help I arrange on my terms." Caleb ran his hand over his jaw. "I need a week to get the cash, so tell your bookie you'll have it by next weekend. Then, you need to lay low."

"I leave for another week out of town on Sunday," he said. "New York. A long ways from Texas."

"I suggest you go sooner," Caleb said. "Get the hell out of town until I get you the money. As in, the first flight out tomorrow."

"I can't," he said. "I have no money for the extra days."

Caleb cursed again. "That entire thousand I gave you is gone?"

"I tried to win back the money," he said.

"I'll meet you at the bank after my jump in the morning to give you something to live on," Caleb said. "But don't let me find out you gambled it away."

Kent held up his hands. "I swear, man. I'm done. I've learned my lesson."

"And every drink is an alcoholic's last," Caleb said. "You have a problem, Kent. You aren't going to get better without help."

"I'll get help," he said. "I'll do whatever you want."

"You're right," Caleb said. "You will." He dug in his pocket and pulled out his wallet and handed Kent what cash he had. He couldn't have Kent stay at his place without Shay flipping out. "Stay in a hotel. I'll go by your house with you after the bank tomorrow, so you can pack."

Kent hung his head. "I don't want Mom and Dad and Shay to find out about this," he said. "Please."

"I'm not going to promise that," Caleb said. "Right now I'm going back to bed. I have an early jump. Meet me at the Hotzone office at nine." Caleb didn't wait for an answer. He headed inside, shut the door and leaned against it. Damn it. He should have come home more often. He should have stayed in touch with Kent. Maybe he would have seen this before it became this kind of problem.

"Caleb?" Shay peeked around the corner.

Caleb heard Kent's truck pulling away, and he motioned her forward. "You're safe. He's gone."

"What's wrong?" she asked, looking nervous, as if she were afraid of the answer, her hands in front of her, fingers twisting together.

His gaze swept her slender body, which was covered in one of his T-shirts. He liked her in his shirt. He loved her. And damn if he didn't want to take her back to bed and work off his frustration, but it wasn't that simple.

He closed the distance between them and took her hand, sitting down on the couch and taking her with him. She curled by his side. "Caleb?"

"Everyone is fine, if that's what's worrying you," he said, kissing her forehead. "Or they will be. Kent is in some trouble." He went on to detail what had been said between him and Kent.

"I have ten thousand saved," Shay said. "I don't have it all, but—"

He squeezed her hand. "I've got the money, Shay, and I don't care about the money. I care about getting Kent right. You're the expert here. What's our best move?"

"A family intervention and a treatment center," she said. "Which hopefully his insurance will cover. It should. I know he has excellent benefits through his company." She hesitated. "Mom and Dad, me and you have to be strong as a unit. We can't do anything to risk that right now."

Tension coiled inside Caleb. "You mean us. You don't want to tell them about us."

"Not until we deal with Kent," she said. "They're going to be devastated. They may overreact to you and I if we do this now. They may just need an emotional outlet and direct it at our relationship. It's human, Caleb." She touched his face. "I don't want to risk them seeing us as a part of something bad going on. I want them to see this as wonderful. Like I do."

Caleb took her hand in his, and he was willing to accept her logic...for now. But he had a gut feeling—and his gut feelings never failed him—there would be another reason to stay silent after this one, and another after that. Until Caleb was forced to say *no more*.

And the very fact that he knew it would come to that had him questioning what she really felt. She said she loved him, but wasn't it a given that she would love him on some level? They *were* family. He loved his fellow Aces. They were family, too—brothers. But did she love him the way he loved her? He didn't know. He didn't know if she knew, either.

15

SHAY WAS AWAKE when Caleb got up to shower and dress for his sunrise jump. They'd gone to bed shortly after Kent had left, and though she'd snuggled close to Caleb's side and he had willingly, if not eagerly, held her, she'd felt the tension radiating off him. She wasn't sure either of them had done more than fade in and out of sleep.

By the time he walked into the bedroom, clean-shaven, his sandy brown hair damp and a bit rumpled, she was sitting up, leaning against the wall, hugging the sheet to her naked body. Her body ached with the pure male appeal he held. But it was her heart that ached with the same tension that had been in bed with them, still thick and present.

"What are you doing awake?" he asked, his surprise evident in his tone.

Shay knew she had to do something to break the chilly ice forming between them, to ease the tension. Something daring and attention-grabbing. "The bed isn't the same without you," she said, and dropped the sheet. "Cancel the jump. Come back to bed with me."

His gaze skimmed her naked body from the waist up and heat flashed in his gaze, but all too quickly banked. He sat down and tugged the sheet to her shoulders. "That's the naughty behavior that'll earn you that spanking." His voice was soft, playful, no evidence of any of that tension. "You know I have customers waiting."

"Stay," she said, "and I'll give you lots of reasons to spank me." She grinned. "We both know you have a kinky spanking fantasy. You bring it up too much not to."

"I have a long list of 'Shay' fantasies," he said. "And it might surprise you to know, they don't all involve sex. You have your 'one hundred things to do' list. I have my 'one hundred things to do with, or to, Shay' list. And that's just in the next few months. After your flying lesson, we'll go to that Mexican joint you like, catch that movie we wanted to see and then I'll show you one or two of the more select picks on my list."

She laughed, her heart feeling lighter already. "I'll trade you one thing off my list for one thing off your list, each day for a hundred days."

He wiggled an eyebrow. "That's a deal I can't refuse."

"I'll go first," she offered. "Now. You want to know the first item on my to-do list?"

"Okay," he said. "I'll bite. What's the first item on your list?"

"I wanted to make love to you no matter where, how or when." She touched his cheek, traced the strong line of his jaw. "I knew someday I'd finally know what it was like to be with you. And I was right. It was too good to miss." Sincerity etched her words, softened her tone. "Good enough to want to repeat every day for the rest of my life."

Caleb went still, his gaze searching her face an instant, before he yanked his shirt off and went down on the bed with her, tugging the sheet away. She laughed. "I thought you had to go to work?"

"Ryan's helping out this morning," he said, spreading her legs and settling between them. "He can handle the jump prep. I have better things *to do*."

Shay laughed again, tightening her arms round his neck. The tension between them was gone and so was next week's deadline for sharing their secret. They had at least a hundred days of bliss all to themselves.

***

AT MIDMORNING, with his jumps behind him for the day, Caleb sat on Kent's brown leather couch, nerves on edge, ready for a fight, as he waited for him to pack. At any moment, he expected the bookie or his men pounding on the door, demanding his cash. Caleb could call the police, but the fight would be over by the time they got here. If the sharks were out, they'd come in if they wanted in, and Caleb would be forced to make sure they turned right back around and left.

The only plus was, Kent's apartment was in the highly populated Arbor area not far from Shay's house, which would discourage a daytime confrontation. Though it was an older apartment lacking a security gate. It ran Kent barely six hundred dollars a month. Caleb knew because he'd looked around for a short-term lease when he'd come back home, something to get him by until he bought a place. The six hundred wasn't much rent, considering Kent made an easy six figures per year and should be investing in owning something.

The furniture was rental, cookie-cutter style, and there wasn't much else to the place besides a few sports pictures and a family photo on the fireplace mantel from Shay's college graduation. Caleb had come home for it, and he and Shay had set off fireworks. He'd barely escaped acting on their attraction. It had been his last trip home for years, afterward he'd shut out everyone, Kent included. Caleb couldn't help but wonder again if he would have seen this coming had he kept in touch.

"I'm ready," Kent said, looking gaunt and tired, as if he hadn't eaten or slept for a few days.

"What time's your flight?"

"Three," he said.

Caleb nodded and stood up. "I'll go to the airport and wait with you."

"You don't have to do that," Kent said. "I'll be okay. They gave me a week to pay and there's security at the airport."

Yeah, Caleb knew how that went. His buddy in the Army had been given time, too, and a good beating as a reminder that the hours were ticking by. Caleb suspected Kent was smart enough to know that was a possibility or he wouldn't have brought up security. "You sitting at the airport with time to find yourself in trouble isn't a good idea."

Kent ran his hand over his jaw. "You got me there."

Caleb motioned to the door. "I'll follow you," he said. "But right now, you follow me outside."

Kent laughed, but without humor. "You don't have to watch over me like this," he said. "I do know how to fight, you know. I seem to remember you and I sparring a time or two."

That was years of training ago, but Caleb didn't want to throw around his skill, verbally or physically—not unless he meant business. So instead, he said, "My Special Forces buddy with ten years of training wasn't worried when he ran up a tab with his bookie, either," he said. "But the four guys with baseball bats whacked some sense into him."

Kent swallowed hard. "I'll follow you out."

Enough said, Caleb gave him a quick incline of his head, and they moved to the parking lot without delay or disturbance. Caleb climbed in his truck to trail Kent and then reached for his phone to call Shay and delay their lunch to an early dinner. Not surprisingly, her voice mail picked up. She was probably in the air for her flying lesson. He tossed the phone on the truck seat in case she called back.

He didn't know what was going on with her. Maybe she'd thought she wanted him, but it had always really been about the forbidden fruit. The fantasy. Her to-do list that included sex with him, suddenly took on a new meaning, and he pounded the steering wheel in a rare display of frustration.

No, this couldn't be about sex. She'd told him she loved him, even before he'd told her he loved her. He'd seen it in her eyes, felt it in her touch. But he'd seen something else, too—fear. He had a lot of training and experience spotting fear. She was scared and the sex was a place for her to hide.

She was running from him, he'd realized once he'd left her this morning, once he had enough space to consider what was happening. She wasn't ready for the commitment that coming out publicly required. Which meant one of two things—he hadn't convinced her he was here to stay and was fully committed to her, or he hadn't made her see how much he loved her.

Perhaps if he could figure out what it was that was scaring her... Because if it wasn't her family, it was him. He ground his teeth. She thought he was going to hurt her, which meant he'd hurt her in the past when he'd shut her out of his life, no matter how good his intentions. He had to prove to her he wouldn't hurt her again. He had a week before her parents returned for him to undo ten years of damage, or he had a bad feeling Shay was going to use her parents like she was using sex—as a shield, a barrier that he couldn't get past. He couldn't let her do that. She meant too much to him.

***

SHAY STOOD ON THE SIDELINES of the airfield as her instructor, Lori Day, an ex-Army pilot turned flight instructor, killed the engine of the Cessna Skyhawk.

"I'm doing it!" Sabrina yelled, jumping out of the plane and running toward Shay after riding up front with Lori to get a feel for what it would be like behind the controls. "What a high. I can't wait to get started."

Shay grinned. "I had a feeling you'd like it."

"How close are you to flying solo?"

"Five hours," Shay said. "I can't wait. Caleb wants to be my first passenger. And since he can fly, I figure if I screw up, he can save us."

"You can always take along a chute," Sabrina laughed.

Lori approached. She was tall and athletic, with striking dark brown eyes and silky raven hair that fell below her shoulders when it wasn't tied back, as it was now.

"I take it you guessed she's a little excited," Lori said, indicating Sabrina with a nod and smiling at Shay.

"I had a tiny hint of a clue," Shay agreed.

"You know what I think?" Sabrina said. "Lori should come to work at the Hotzone, and we could offer flight lessons."

Lori held up her hands. "Oh, no. I'm happy right where I'm at."

"We do Special Ops training," Sabrina said. "A pilot would be a great addition."

"I thought the Aces all knew how to fly?" Shay asked. "And they have pilots on staff."

"Which makes a flight school a perfect addition," Sabrina said. "I'm going to talk to Ryan." She eyed Lori. "And be prepared to be propositioned."

Lori snorted. "I was a woman in the Army," she said. "A proposition is like a cup of coffee. A part of waking up." She motioned to the building. "I have to go catch up with my next client."

Shay and Sabrina fell into step behind her. "You want to grab some lunch?" Sabrina asked.

"I would, but Caleb and I have plans for lunch and a movie," she said. "But maybe next weekend after our first lesson. You are coming back next weekend, right?"

"You bet," Sabrina said. "Maybe we can arrange afternoon classes so Jennifer can come. We can make it a threesome."

Shay's stomach did a funny flutter. She loved Caleb. She liked Sabrina. She had no idea why she hesitated to embed herself in the "threesome" of Aces women, why she couldn't feel like she belonged.

Shay eyed her cell phone. "I missed a call from Caleb." She held up a finger and pushed the recall button, worried about Kent. *"Hey, sweetheart. Taking Kent to the airport. I don't want to leave him alone before his flight. I'll be back to the trailer about three-thirty, and I'll be starving. For you and that Mexican food."*

Shay smiled and ended the voice mail, when her phone rang again instantly, and she frowned at the unknown number. "Sorry," she whispered to Sabrina and motioned them onward to the building.

Shay hit Answer as they walked and before she could say hello, she heard, "Doc, it's George. I'm getting married."

"Married?" she blurted, stopping in her footsteps. "Where are you?"

"I'm still in Mexico," he said. "On a boat. We're saying 'I do' in about twenty minutes. No guests. Just me, Anabella and a preacher. Anabella has a big family, but she understands I don't, so we are doing this alone. I've asked her to come to a session when we get back."

"Oh," Shay said, feeling a little relieved that this Anabella woman was willing to support George. "Of course. Call me when you're ready." She drew a breath. "George. This is very fast. Are you sure you shouldn't wait?"

"When you're in love," George said, "you know it. You want to scream it from the rooftops. Why in the world would I wait?" He hung up. Shay stopped walking. She stood there, a few steps from the flight school doorway. and replayed the words. *When you're in love, you know it. Why would you wait?*

"Everything okay?" Sabrina asked.

Shay shook off the unsettled feeling in her stomach. She smiled at Sabrina. "Fine. One of my patients with happy news."

"Oh," Sabrina said. "It didn't sound so happy." She shrugged. "You have time for coffee in the snack bar?"

"Sure," Shay said and followed Sabrina inside.

"Good," Sabrina, her eyes lighting. "I want to hear about that sudden exit you and Caleb made last night. The steam coming off you two was downright scorching. Oh, and what happened with Kent when he caught you out at the Hotzone?" She snagged Shay's arm. "Let's talk."

Shay cringed. She didn't want to talk about last night any more than she wanted to think about George's comment.

Nevertheless, she found herself sitting across from Sabrina and sipping an iced mocha a few minutes later.

"I needed this," Shay said. "Both the caffeine and the cold drink."

Sabrina wiggled a dark brow. "Not much sleep last night?"

"Taking advantage of every minute until my parents get back from Italy," Shay explained, and then wondered why the heck she had said it. What happened to not wanting to talk about this?

Sabrina studied her a moment. "And what happens when they come back?"

"Back to sneaking around to see Caleb," Shay said.

"I take it Kent didn't figure out what's going on then?"

Shay shook her head. "No. We told him I was going to jump and then chickened out."

Sabrina studied her another long moment. Shay shifted under the scrutiny.

"What?" Shay asked.

"Is that really a relief? Kent not finding out? I mean, wasn't there a part of you that just wanted the romance to be out of the closet?"

"It's complicated, Sabrina."

"So you keep saying."

"But it is."

"No," Sabrina said. "It's not. Do you love Caleb?"

"Yes."

"Okay then," Sabrina said. "Complication dissolved. That's all that matters."

But she was wrong. So wrong. Most people didn't fall in love with a man who called *her* family *his* family. What happened if... She swallowed hard, shoving aside the what-ifs and a deeper fear that gnawed at her and refused to take form. She didn't want it to take form. She didn't want to know what it was, because it didn't matter. She *did* love Caleb. They would get through this, right after they dealt with Kent. When the time was right.

Not today. Today, she didn't have to think about it. Today, she and Caleb were going to that dinner and movie, and then indulging in one of his hundred fantasies. Just the two of them—just the here and now.

16

THE SATURDAY AFTER Kent's surprise visit to Caleb's trailer, Shay stood at the living room window of her parents' house and stared out at the rain pelting down on the ground, waiting for her parents' cab to arrive. They'd insisted her car was too small for their bags, and Caleb's truck only had room in the back, which wasn't covered.

Caleb stepped behind her, framing her body with his, his hands on her hips. "You're vibrating with nerves," he said, his hands running down her shoulders.

Shay leaned against him, and shut her eyes. "I hate we have to tell them about Kent the minute they walk in the door."

"I know," he said. "But we can't put this off. Not with Kent in this kind of trouble."

Shay rotated in his arms. "Can't we turn back the clock and live this past week all over again?" It had been one of the best weeks of her life. They'd managed to put aside the impending troubles with Kent and her parents, and enjoy each other.

They'd even started to get little routines: they knew what time she got home, what time he got home. And Tuesday and Wednesday had been dinner in the living room to watch *American Idol*. Chinese takeout, Tuesday; pizza, Wednesday. Caleb said *Idol* was a guilty pleasure so opposite to how he'd spent the last ten years of his life that he couldn't deny himself. She loved that there were many sides to him. And then there was bedtime, and the countdown through the hundred to-do items.

"There's always next week," he promised. "And the next. We just need to get this behind us. Behind Kent."

"I know," she agreed. "But maybe we shouldn't have Kent coming over just yet." They'd told Kent they were having a welcome-home dinner for his parents, instead of the intervention they had planned. "Not until we know how Mom and Dad are going to react to what's going on. What if they aren't supportive of a treatment program?"

"Is it what's best for Kent?"

"Well, yes, but—"

"Can you, as a professional, assure them it's the right thing for Kent?"

"Yes, but—"

He kissed her to shut her up, a fast, full-mouth kiss. "Then they'll trust you. I do."

Shay wrapped her arms around his neck. "Thank you," she said. "And thank you for what you're doing for Kent."

"If you want to thank me," he said, running his hand over her hip and caressing one jean-clad butt cheek, "I'll give you a reason to thank me tonight. But don't thank me for taking care of Kent. He'd do the same for me if things were reversed."

"I should have seen this," she said. "I'm a trained professional. I mean the signs were there, Caleb. In grade school before you were even around, he'd bet his school lunch money on stupid stuff like what color of shirt a teacher would wear that day, or what grade someone would get on a test. And you know the way he was in high school. He held betting pools on who'd go to prom with who."

"That betting pool became famous by the time he was a senior," he said. "I even think a few teachers secretly participated. His senior pot was three grand. That's big money for a high school kid. And he got two dollars for every bet placed. At that point, I was sure he was going to end up a millionaire. Instead he's flat broke."

"And now you're almost flat broke," she said, and frowned.

He shrugged off the comment in a way that made her curious. "Aren't you?" she asked.

"Do you really want to know?"

She gaped. "Good grief, Caleb. How much money *did* you make on those investments?" She held out her hands. "Not that it matters but—well, how much?"

Tenderness slid into his voice, his expression softening. "Enough for at least one more romantic trip to Italy for two. For you and me, Shay."

"What?" she whispered, her throat raspy, suddenly dry. Italy? It was a beautiful nightmare. One she'd never recover from if he pulled back again.

The front door opened. "Hello! Hello!"

Shay panicked and instinctively shoved out of Caleb's arms. Their eyes locked and held, and she watched the affection in his expression bleed away. Shay's heart stuttered, and she stepped toward him. "Caleb, I didn't mean to seem... I want to tell them the right way, the right time." She could see her words hadn't changed his reaction. "Please. Please don't be angry."

"Shay! Caleb!" Her mother's voice grew closer, until it was in the doorway of the living room. "Oh, my goodness, it's coming down out there. Caleb, honey, can you help your father? He's riding the bags up the driveway like boats."

Caleb cut his gaze from Shay, and there was no mistaking his unhappiness, or the sudden icy chill in the air.

"Caleb—" she began, trying to make things right, but he cut her off, answering Sharon instead.

"On my way," he called, leaving Shay without another glance. The instant Caleb was within Sharon's reach, Sharon grabbed him and hugged him. "It was the best two weeks of my life. Thank you, Caleb."

Shay watched Caleb's face as he hugged her mother. His eyes were shut, but his jaw was tense, the handsomely rugged lines of his face strained. Because of her, she thought guiltily. But when he pulled back to look at Sharon, he smiled, and it transformed his features, as if the harshness of moments before had never existed. "I can't wait to hear all about the trip," he said.

A grumble followed by a rant of cursing came from the doorway. Shay's father had made it to the house but not happily. Sharon grimaced. "You better help. He's an old man, Caleb. He really might float away."

Caleb chuckled and went to do as ordered. Shay rushed forward and hugged her mother, leaning back to ask, "So Italy was amazing?"

"A fairy tale," she said. "I still can't believe Caleb did that for us." She waved at Shay, already walking. "Come to the kitchen and let me show you what I brought you."

Fifteen minutes later, Shay's mother was talking a million miles an hour, with wine and all kinds of cookbooks, and yummy treats for Shay, Caleb and Kent. And Shay wanted to hear it all, she wanted to be excited with her mother. A hard thing to do, between Caleb's being upset with her and the dread over telling her parents about Kent. Shay's stomach was churning, the memory of the IHOP brunch she and Caleb had indulged in earlier in the day ever present, and not nearly as pleasant now as it had been to eat.

In the next room, Shay could hear Bob telling Caleb about the trip, talking more than she thought she'd heard her father talk in years. All this happiness and excitement, and Shay and Caleb were about to twist them in knots. And soon. It had to be soon or Kent would arrive and they wouldn't be ready for him.

As if he'd been reading her mind, Caleb appeared in the doorway of the kitchen. "Sharon," he said, "Shay and I have something we need to sit down and discuss with you and Bob." He paused, but his tone had been grave, his expression stark as he added, "Before Kent gets here."

Sharon set down the package of pasta in her hand. "Oh, my. Is everything okay?"

Shay touched her mother's back. "It's fine," she said, and offered a reassuring smile. "We just need to have a little family problem-solving powwow," she said. "Something we didn't want to hit you with the day you came home, but unfortunately, it's necessary."

Once they were all gathered around the coffee table—Shay and her mother on the couch, Caleb and her father in the leather chairs across from them—Shay glanced at Caleb, and he explained what had happened with Kent. Then, as planned, Shay showed her parents some brochures for a treatment facility she'd checked out for Kent, and explained what she felt, professionally, needed to be done. She'd consulted several peers, as this was personal, and she wanted to be sure she was objective.

Neither of her parents said much as Shay and Caleb talked. Shay sat back, hands on her legs, and said, "When he gets here, we'd like to talk to him. Use the power of a family intervention to insist he get help."

Sharon covered her face with her hands and sobbed. Shay hugged her, her gaze seeking Caleb's. "Sharon," Caleb offered, "Kent is safe. We just want to keep him that way. And if he keeps gambling like this, there's going to come a point where I can't bail him out."

"You'll get every damn dime back," Bob said, his voice crackling with emotion masked by out-of-character anger. "If I have to pay you myself."

Caleb reached over and patted Bob's shoulder. "I don't want your money. I don't give a damn about the money. I care about Kent. These men he's involved with are not people you mess with."

"When can he check into this place?" Sharon asked urgently. "I want him locked away someplace safe. Can he go tonight?"

Shay and Caleb exchanged a look. They had agreement on the treatment facility. That was a major step in the right direction. "He needs time to arrange things with his work and his insurance, and they can't get him in for two weeks anyway. Not at this facility, which is not only close, in the Hill Country, but well-respected. We'll just have to keep an eye on him the next two weeks and make sure he doesn't go running up another debt."

"We have to start by getting his agreement to check himself into the treatment facility," Caleb reminded everyone.

"He'll go," Bob said. "If I have to drag him there kicking and screaming, he'll go."

"He will have to stay with you until he checks in, Caleb," Sharon said. "Then he'll be safe. You and your Army friends can keep him in line, if anyone can. Please, Caleb. He has to stay with you. I won't rest if he's not with you, protected."

Caleb's expression didn't change, but Shay saw the barely perceivable flex of his jaw, the tension climbing down his spine as he stiffened slightly. "Let's see how it goes with Kent, and we'll do what we have to. Why don't we give you guys a few minutes to talk alone? This is a lot to absorb." Slowly, his attention shifted to Shay. "Let's get some air."

Shay gave a jerky nod, made sure her mother was okay and then followed Caleb to the back patio. The minute they were outside, he grabbed her hand and pulled her around the corner, out of sight and out of their hearing.

"We have to tell your parents about us if Kent's going to stay with me," he said. "There's no way we can keep us a secret under those circumstances. Not without completely staying away from each other."

"We'll be careful," she said. "We'll make it work. It's only two weeks."

His hands settled on his hips, frustration etching his brow. "Make it work," he repeated. "That's your answer?"

Shay's heart thundered in her chest. "We can't spring our relationship on my parents right now. Can't you see how upset they are?"

"Funny," he said. "I'm not so sure they'll be upset we're together. But you, on the other hand, are convinced they will be. You know what I think? I think this isn't about your parents at all. I think it's about something else, and you're using them as an excuse."

"No," Shay said instantly. "You're wrong. That's crazy, Caleb. There isn't something else. There isn't."

"There is," he said with certainty. "I saw it in your face when I brought up Italy, and every time I bring up telling Bob and Sharon that we're a couple."

"Kent's here," Bob called from the doorway.

"You know, Shay," he said, "maybe these two weeks are what we need. What you need to figure out what I am to you. Because I know what you are to me. The woman I love. The only woman I've ever said that to. You need to figure out what I am to you. The man you love or that forbidden fantasy you talked about." He gave the door a nod. "Let's go give Kent the attention he needs to get well."

He stepped around her and headed to the house, leaving Shay to stare after him. Leaving her alone. She struggled with the coldness of the feeling, the desire to go after him and make things right somehow, make him understand that she was protecting him. She was making sure bad timing didn't induce a negative reaction from her family about their relationship—about him. There *wasn't* another reason behind her silence.

Shay forced herself into a jog to catch up with Caleb and entered the living room just behind him to find Kent standing with her parents.

"Why do I get the feeling this isn't a homecoming party?" Kent asked.

Probably because her parents sat side by side on the couch, silent and tense, with pinched looks on their faces.

"Because it's not," Caleb said, his tone no-nonsense, as if he were talking to a young soldier about to face his first enemy-combat situation. "Why don't you grab a seat and let's chat."

"You told them," Kent said.

"Absolutely, I told them," Caleb agreed, owning his actions in a way that only made Shay respect him more.

Kent's gaze locked with Caleb's and stiff seconds ticked by, a male standoff of some sort Shay didn't try to understand. Finally, Kent slumped slightly, conceding the control to Caleb, and skulked to a chair to sit.

"You have a gambling problem, Kent," Caleb said, "and don't tell us you're going to stop and you have it under control. Because you won't and you don't." Authority oozed out of Caleb. He was strong and forceful, without being disrespectful. "So here's what's going to happen. We're going to pay off your debt tonight, and then you'll stay with me to detour any further temptation until you can check in to a rehab facility. Shay's done preliminary research to find the right place, one she believes your insurance will cover." He paused and added, "That's it. This is nonnegotiable."

Shay held her breath, waiting for Kent's response, and she could see her parents were doing the same. Several seconds ticked by, before Kent asked, "Where exactly is this facility?"

The tension in the room eased instantly, as if everyone let out that held breath all at once, and Shay glanced at Caleb's profile in admiration. His strength, and his absolute resolve that Kent get help, had made this happen. Kent was going to get better, and she wasn't sure it would have happened so easily if Caleb hadn't been home.

Shay stepped forward and sat next to Kent, grabbing the brochure and explaining everything to him. A few minutes later, Kent nodded. "I'll do it. I..." His voice cracked and Shay realized he was crying. Kent. Her big, badass brother cried. And so did her big, badass father. Shay and her mother followed.

Caleb stood above them all, a silent source of strength. The room fed off of it, the pillar in a world that wobbled left and right, and steadied in the center—with him. Shay knew she did.

A knock sounded at the door, and Shay cast Caleb an inquiring look. He glanced at the clock on the mantel. "Right on time," he said, and headed to the door.

He returned with Bobby and Ryan by his side. Shay swallowed hard at the sight they made, the three men standing there, all tall, broad and foreboding. For the first time, Shay realized they were lethal. Not that she hadn't known. They were Special Forces. But standing there, aligned together in readiness, they were both frightening and magnificent.

"Let's go see your bookie," Caleb said to Kent.

Kent pushed to his feet. "I'm ready." He walked to stand with the other men, and Ryan and Bobby gave him room to fall into the lineup next to Caleb. Instantly, Kent stood a little stronger, his demeanor more confident and determined. Shay's heart squeezed at the strength that having Caleb around gave him, gave them all.

"Call us when you get back to Caleb's place," Sharon ordered.

"I'll call," Kent said. "And I'll be okay."

Caleb motioned to Shay to follow him outside, and relief fluttered through her. Good. He wasn't shutting her out. Shay stepped onto the front porch as Bobby and Ryan climbed in one vehicle and Kent climbed behind the wheel of his own truck.

Caleb handed her his keys. "Take my truck," he said. "Kent will drop me by later to pick it up." He turned away.

Shay stepped toward him and touched his arm. "Caleb, wait." He glanced over his shoulder, didn't even turn back to her. She swallowed hard and said, "Be careful."

He gave her a steely stare and nodded before stepping out of her reach, again, leaving her alone. And this time, she wasn't so sure she wasn't going to stay that way.

17

KENT PULLED INTO Shay's driveway, and Caleb shoved open the passenger's door and hesitated. He didn't want to talk to Shay right now. He needed space, some time to think, but he wasn't up to playing nice in front of Kent, either. "I'll just grab the keys, and then we can go. I know you're anxious to get to the trailer and get settled, but hang tight, will you? If you're waiting for me, Shay'll have to tame the question-and-answer session I'm sure is headed my way."

"You want me to come in with you?" Kent asked.

"The idea is to get out of here quickly," Caleb reminded him. "You wait, with the truck running."

"Copy that," Kent said. "Good luck with the twenty questions."

Caleb slammed the door and headed to Shay's front porch about the time she appeared in the entryway. Instinctively, the male part of him responded, the part that wanted Shay more than he wanted his next breath. His gaze swept her navy blue sweats and then the light blue-and-navy T-shirt that hugged her high breasts and accented her narrow waist. Caleb silently cursed his raging hormones and the damn stretch of his zipper.

"Is Kent okay?" she asked eagerly, glancing over her shoulder to the running truck, headlights on dim.

"Everything is fine," he said. "The bookie is paid, and he knows Kent won't be back for more action."

Discouraging conversation, he got to the point. "I came for my keys."

"Come in while I grab them," she said, stepping back to let him in. He didn't move, and she whispered, "Please."

Forcing himself to make eye contact, he regretted it the moment he did. Her eyes were as blue as her shirt, a mixture of sea and sky, torment and hope, that he yearned to unravel and understand.

Caleb shoved his hands in his pockets, so he wouldn't touch her. "We both know that's not a good idea."

She stepped forward, started to touch him and hugged herself instead. The scent of perfume and Shay created a powerful drag on his willpower.

"I don't want to spend two weeks without you," she said. "I don't want to spend tonight without you."

"But you're willing," he said.

"Because it's necessary," she added. "My father cried, Caleb. My father. The timing is wrong."

"Maybe," he conceded. "And if I believed for a minute that was really what was going on between us, I'd accept that answer. But I don't. I get that you're not comfortable going public. And I'm not comfortable running around like some school kid with his hand in the cookie jar. And frankly, at this point, if you told me you wanted to go public, I'd say no because *I'd know* you did it because I'd pressured you. I don't want you like that, any more than I want to sneak around." He ran his hand over his hair. "I need the keys, Shay. And we need some space to think."

She stared at him, her blue eyes glistening, more powerful than any enemy's weapon he'd ever faced. She turned away and not a second too soon. Caleb had no idea how he kept from reaching for her. She returned with the keys and walked straight up to stand in front of him. Close. So close that her unique scent, all feminine and floral, flared in his nostrils, warming him...all but demanding he bury his face in her neck and then kiss her.

She took his hand and pressed the keys to his palm, staring down at their joined hands. "I do love you, Caleb."

"We've always loved each other, Shay," he said softly. "It just never seems to be our time." He untangled his hands from hers and walked away. And she let him. She let him because her brother was watching. Actions spoke volumes, beyond words.

***

SHAY SPENT THE NIGHT tossing and turning, miserable without Caleb, tormented by his insistence they should take these two weeks to "think." She'd picked up the phone countless times to call him. Cried. Paced. Took a hot bath. Paced some more. And then she got angry. By morning her helplessness had transformed to outright fire, and she knew she had to take action.

Being Sunday morning, Shay knew Caleb would have a sunrise jump. She pulled into the Hotzone parking lot a little past nine, when she knew he'd be finishing up.

She walked into the office and found Sabrina behind the desk, which meant Ryan was working. "Hey, Shay," she said. "I didn't know you were coming, too, this morning. Before long, Caleb will be sweet-talking you into covering the front desk, like Ryan to does me."

Doubtful, thought Shay, but instead she said, "I'm not a morning person, so he'll be surprised to see me."

She tried to smile, but it just didn't happen. "Where is he?"

"He should be pulling up any minute in one of the jeeps," she said. "The plane's already returned." She frowned. "Everything okay?"

"Ask me after I talk to Caleb," she said, and she didn't wait for an answer. Shay headed to the back door where she could get to the four operating hangars, knowing Caleb's jeep would pull up behind the first.

She squinted against the new sun piercing the horizon, the air already hot and sticky enough to make her jeans and T-shirt feel overdressed. A jeep appeared in the distance, and Shay tracked its path, noting three men inside.

Caleb parked the jeep with two customers inside. Another jeep barreled up behind it, but Shay looked right through it. She had Caleb in sight, and she suddenly felt hotter than hot, and it had nothing to do with the sun. She was ticked.

Shay charged toward Caleb as he rounded the jeep, and damn him, he looked good enough to eat in his flight suit. Surprise flickered in his face when he saw her, and he murmured something to the men, who headed toward the building.

"We have to talk," she said, coming almost toe-to toe with him, her chin lifting to allow a good, heartfelt glare. "Now. Today."

"Then you'll have to jump. I have several customers waiting."

"Jump?" she declared, her anger replaced by panic.

From behind, Shay heard, "What's up, Shay?"

She recognized Kent's voice before he appeared by their side, dressed in a flight suit to match Caleb's. Shay cringed. She should have guessed Caleb would bring Kent to jump today.

Caleb answered, "Shay's jumping."

"No way are you jumping," Kent said. "I'll believe it when I see it."

Ryan walked by with several customers on his heels. He gave Shay a nod and waved Kent forward. "If you're going up with me again, bring your ass on."

Caleb tugged Shay forward. Shay dug in her heels. "I'm not jumping."

He turned to her and hugged her close. "Jump with me, Shay."

There was something about the way he said it, the way he was looking at her, that made her forget Kent might be watching. As if he were asking her for more than a skydiving jump. Her chest tightened. "I'm scared."

He brushed hair out of her eyes and stared down at her. "I know," he said. "Maybe one day you won't be. Maybe one day you'll be ready to jump." He released her, and turned and jogged toward the building. And again, Shay stood staring after him. Alone. Trying to understand what had just happened, because she was pretty sure neither of them had been talking about skydiving.

***

THREE EVENINGS LATER, Shay was still at work at seven, having long ago moved to her couch, kicked off her black heels and stacked files on the coffee table for easy access. And with her feet tucked by her side, her black skirt above the knees—modesty of little concern since she'd long ago sent her secretary home and she was alone—she was determined to catch up on paperwork. And if she were honest with herself, which wasn't exactly her current preference, she was avoiding going home alone—translation: without Caleb—for a few more hours.

At present, though, Shay ended a call with the treatment center Kent would be checking into, his arrangements finalized for a week from Saturday. Eager to share the news, Shay dialed Kent. Disappointingly, he didn't answer, and she left a detailed message. He was eager to get this behind him, and she wanted him to know he was one step closer. Shay hesitated and considered calling Caleb, but then set the phone down as if burned.

She hadn't heard from him, not since he'd asked her to jump with him and she'd told him she was scared. Ever since, well...she didn't know what to say to him, and clearly he didn't have anything to say to her. She didn't even remember exactly what she'd planned to say to him when she'd charged up to him and demanded they talk. Something along the lines of "Damn it, why do you get to say when it's the right or wrong time for us?" At least, she thought that was the general idea. Her mind was too cluttered to be certain. All she knew was she missed him. And she was, indeed, scared, and she wasn't even completely sure why.

The idea of figuring it out had Shay snatching a file to read. She would not think about Caleb. She'd get her work done. It was the strategy that had gotten her past the last few days. It would get her through tonight. Exhaustion certainly helped lessen the pain of sleeping alone in a bed with his scent all over it.

Not ten minutes later though, her phone rang. Assuming it was Kent, she answered without checking caller ID.

"Doc," came the male sob.

Shay sat up straight, the file in her lap tumbling to the ground. "What's wrong, George?"

"I want to see Jessie again," he said, referring to his dead wife.

Shay went completely still, realizing George was no longer happy, and he was absolutely not okay. Her worst fear had come true. Something in this new relationship had gone horribly wrong. "Jessie is with you, George," she said. "Remember we've talked about this. Jessie is watching out for you."

"I don't want her to watch me anymore," he said, and this time it was clear he was crying. "I want to touch her and hold her and smell the scent of her on my skin. I need her. I'm going to see her."

Shay stood up and struggled to get her shoes on, admitting that George had reverted to a dangerous emotional place she'd hoped they were long past. "George," she said urgently. "Are you at home? Where are you? I'll come to you."

"The Hyatt Regency downtown," he said. "On the roof." He hung up.

Shay ran for her purse and keys and dialed information as she headed to the hallway. She took the stairs for speed and cell-phone reception, and asked the customer service rep at the Hyatt for the manager of the hotel.

"What's this regarding?" the woman asked.

"It's an emergency," she said. "I'm a doctor. One of my patients is there, and..." She stopped. She had no way of knowing if George was really suicidal. And alerting the police might not be the best option. She had a close colleague who'd once had a patient threaten to kill himself. He'd hidden in a field of high grass with a rifle. Her colleague had called the police, and the patient had pulled the trigger when one of the cops was in the grass a few feet from finding him. To this day, that colleague was convinced that calling the police had pushed her patient over the edge. Shay hung up the phone, sick to her stomach with the possibility that it was the wrong choice not to alert the hotel.

"They'd have called the police," she whispered. At the bottom of the stairwell, she ran to her car and didn't even wait for the car to stop before she switched from Reverse and slammed it in forward gear. She jerked into motion and fretfully contemplated her options.

By the time she reached the highway headed downtown, she could think of only one person who could help.

Shay dialed her phone, praying Caleb would answer. Praying he wasn't on a sunset jump. He answered on the third ring. "Hello, Shay," he said.

His voice was warm, encouraging, and it opened a floodgate for Shay. "My patient...George—I think he might be about to try to commit suicide, but I'm afraid to call the police...in case that pushes him to actually do it. He wouldn't have called me if he didn't want to be stopped. I'm going to him now, but I—"

"Where is he?" Caleb said. "And where are you?"

"He says he's on the roof of the downtown Hyatt, off Sixth Street. I'm halfway there."

"I know where it's at," he said, "and I'm already walking to my truck."

She let out a breath of relief. "Thank you, Caleb."

"It'll be okay, Shay," he said. "I'll see you in a few minutes." He hung up, and Shay breathed just a little easier through the remaining ten-minute drive.

Shay pulled into the Hyatt parking lot and took the stairs to the lobby level. After a tortuously long elevator ride, another set of stairs sent her and her high heels into blister-and-gasp territory, but she heaved through it. She burst through the door of the roof, and stopped abruptly. George was there all right, standing with his back to her, his feet dangerously close to the edge of the building.

Terror gripped Shay. It would be so easy for George to go over that ledge. And so easy for her to say or do the wrong thing that it was almost paralyzing. The minute she began interacting, the reactions would begin. The chance for error would exist.

Behind her, the door creaked. A second later, Caleb stepped to her side. He glanced at George, and if he was rattled, he didn't show it, didn't so much as blink. He turned toward her, and lifted the blue-jean jacket he wore, to display a harness strap with rope attached, she assumed he planned to use it to link himself with George. The very fact that Caleb wasn't unprepared to take action was comforting as long as she didn't think about how Caleb might actually try to get that harness on George and how easily he might go over the wall with George in the process.

Caleb wrapped his arm around her and pulled her close, the unique scent of him invading her senses, a comforting scent she inhaled, as he whispered, "Get me to that ledge with him. Tell him I'm a friend you called for moral support. Make sure he knows I'm not with the authorities."

Her hand pressed to his chest, the heat and sound of his heartbeat radiating comfort. She nodded, and he ran his hand down her hair. "Take a deep breath, sweetheart, and trust your instincts. You'll be fine and so will he."

Shay absorbed the words, and let her determination form. She was getting George off that ledge. She started walking, watching George closely as she approached. He wasn't a large man—five foot nine and a hundred and fifty pounds dripping wet by her estimate. Often she'd thought of him as effeminate and a bit frail. But standing on that ledge, his spine stiff, he looked bigger, more confident than usual. Almost as if he were empowered, ready to jump.

She was only a few feet away from him when he turned, his gaze shooting to Caleb. "Who is he? Who'd you bring with you?"

"I'm a friend," Caleb said, easing closer. "Shay called me when she was on her way over here, said she needed me. She was worried and didn't want to call the police."

"What kind of friend?" George asked suspiciously.

Caleb stopped beside Shay and shoved his hands in his pockets, giving her a quick look before answering. "I'll just say this...about three days ago she had me ready to stand on that ledge by your side. Who put *you* up there?"

"Anabella," he said. "She wanted me for the money I inherited from my Jessie. She knew Jessie. She knew about the money."

Caleb said, "That's when you tell her you only wanted her for the sex, and it wasn't that damn good anyway. I mean it's not like you knew her long, right? What else could it have been about?"

George actually laughed, the intensity in him dropping a good two notches. "I wish I had it in me to think of snappy comebacks like that." He turned somber. "I thought I loved her."

"So the sex was good?" Caleb asked. "Because good sex has a way of doing that." Caleb turned to Shay. "And no, we aren't about sex. At least it's not about sex to me." He eyed George. "You're about to get me in trouble."

George grinned at Shay. "Is it about sex to you?"

"No!" she said.

"But it's good, right?" Caleb asked.

Shay could feel her face redden. “Okay, both of you. This isn’t the time or place to be talking about this. George. Come down right now. I can’t talk to you while you’re standing there.”

He shook his head. “No. No, I can’t.”

She softened. “Anabella might seem like a mistake to you,” she said, “but she woke you up, George. She made you live life again.”

“I don’t want to live again,” he said. “It hurts.”

“And it feels good,” Shay said. “That’s the joy. You appreciate the good because of the bad. You don’t want to jump, George. You want to live.”

“You know what I do when I want to jump,” Caleb said.

“What?” George asked eagerly.

“I jump,” he said. “Out of a plane. I skydive.”

George’s eyes went wide. “Skydive,” he said. “That’s crazy. What if the chute doesn’t open?”

“You don’t have a chute standing on that ledge,” Caleb said. “The way I look at skydiving is...if I’m supposed to survive—if I still have a purpose on this earth—the chute will open. If not, then it won’t.” George looked intrigued, and Caleb quickly offered, “I own a skydiving operation in San Marcus. If you want to test my chute theory, we can go now. You can watch some videos and do a little paperwork, and then jump in a few hours. And you’ll have your answer—to live or not to live.”

George looked at Shay. “Will you jump with me?”

Shay’s breath lodged in her throat. Both men stared at her, waiting for an answer to the same question Caleb had asked days before. Would she jump?

18

WILL YOU JUMP WITH ME?

George's question hung in the air like a hammer about to drop. Caleb had done a lot of thinking about why he'd pressed Shay to jump with him three days before, because he wasn't one to push people out of their comfort zone, certainly not Shay. At least, not outside the bedroom. And now, here, in this moment, he knew why. He'd wanted something to show him that, while she might not be willing to tell her family about their relationship, he was worth a risk, worth fighting for. But she hadn't jumped, she hadn't even stayed to talk to him after his jump.

"I'm terrified to jump, George," she said, holding her patient's stare. "But if it will get you down from there, I'll do it."

George scrutinized her, as if deciding whether he should believe her, before jumping to the ground in front of Caleb and Shay. "I'm ready," he told Caleb, and started walking toward the door.

Shay's gaze shifted to Caleb's, trepidation in her expression. "I had to say yes."

"I know," he said. And he did know. That had been the entire point of asking her to jump. He'd wanted her to make a choice—in his case, not to save his life but to save their relationship. To be willing to step out of her comfort zone, a way to reach out to him that she'd not been willing to offer. Maybe it was wrong of him, probably it was wrong of him, but he needed to know.

And, well, he would risk anything for her, but he wasn't sure it would be enough anymore.

His lips thinned with the thought and he said, "George is waiting."

Once they were in the parking lot, Caleb wasn't about to let George out of their sight until he was certain he was stable. Nor was he leaving George alone with Shay. He'd seen a few suicidal guys in Iraq turn on people close to them. "Let's take my truck," Caleb suggested. "That'll let you two talk, and neither of you will have the distraction of driving."

Fortunately, George agreed, and was soon seated by the passenger's door, pulling it shut, while Shay scooted to the middle. Caleb climbed into the driver's seat beside Shay, but he didn't look at her. He could feel her close, her body heat rushing over him, her scent teasing him, and that was enough. She was where he'd wanted her. Where he'd believed she belonged. Still did, but now...well, now he wasn't so sure that was where she would end up.

The drive was short and Shay kept George talking. Caleb was impressed with how she framed her views, how she led him to see logic over emotion.

Once inside the Hotzone, Caleb led George and Shay to a private training room and set up the videos to allow George to complete the paperwork to jump alone.

"Shay's jumping tandem with me," Caleb said without asking Shay. "She doesn't need all the paperwork you will need." Shay was scared, and he wasn't risking her getting hurt by forcing her to jump alone.

Shay's gaze connected with his, the charge of awareness and tension between them damn near combustible. There was no way George didn't notice.

George frowned. “But I can for sure jump on my own?” he confirmed, sitting down at the metal table.

“That’s right,” Caleb agreed. “But it’s going to be pretty late by the time you finish all the training. I need to go lock in a pilot for the plane.” His gaze flickered over Shay’s slim-cut skirt, with miles of gorgeous legs exposed from beneath, and added, “And I’ll need to find Shay something to wear. High heels and skydiving don’t mesh too well.”

Shay looked down at herself. “I can’t believe I didn’t think of that. Do I need to run home and change?”

“No,” George said. “You can’t leave me here.”

“Sabrina and Jennifer both have flight suits and boots here,” he said. “You’re are all close to the same size. I’m sure neither will mind if you wear theirs.” He tapped the table where George sat. “You study and before long, I’ll show you what jumping is really all about.”

He motioned to Shay to follow him, pulling the door shut behind him once they were in the hall. “I need to line up that pilot.” He didn’t give her time to respond. The rawness of her rejection of days before had worn on him, tormented him. He turned away.

She reached for him, the touch of her hand jolting him in a way no woman should ever be able to jolt a man.

“Caleb,” she said.

Unnerved by how much Shay got under his skin, he didn’t give her time to voice whatever she’d hoped to say. “You know where the storage room is, right?”

“I...” She hesitated, apparently changing her mind about what she’d been about to say. “Yes. I know where it is.”

“Grab something to change into while I line up what I need to for the jump.” He left, going in search of Ryan, who, in his usually easygoing way, had already agreed to join their jump—if they could get a pilot to hang around.

He found Ryan and Bobby in Bobby's office, just back from a sunset jump. "We got a pilot?" he asked Ryan.

Ryan cast him a grim look. "No go," he said. "Everyone has plans."

Caleb eyed Bobby. "Can you fly us out for a jump, man?"

"If you can't get someone else," Bobby said, "I'll do it. But tonight is Jennifer's mom's birthday, and her dad's planned a surprise party."

"Damn," Caleb murmured.

"I can fly you out," Ryan said. "I'm sure we can get one of the other instructors to help with George."

"This guy was on a ledge about to jump a few hours ago," he said. "If he decides not to pull his chute, someone has to pull it for him. Ryan's the man for that job."

Ryan grinned. "You know I do love a little extra action with my dirt dives."

"What's J.C.'s excuse for not staying?" he asked, referring to their most senior pilot, an old Army buddy of Bobby's.

"Would you believe he has defensive driving?" Bobby asked. "I know. Not comforting that he needs it, considering he's our lead pilot."

"Damn it," Caleb said, running his hand over his face and thought of their newest pilot. "What about Mark?"

"Sent him home early today, and he's not answering his phone," Ryan said.

"I might know someone," Shay said from the doorway.

Caleb turned to find Shay still dressed in her skirt and heels. "Not you," he said.

"Of course not," she said. "I don't have my license yet. But my instructor does, and she's retired Air Force. Sabrina knows her."

"Is that Lori Dew?" Ryan asked.

"Lori Day," Shay corrected.

"Right," Ryan said. "Sabrina talked to me about her, trying to convince me we should hire her and add flight lessons to the Hotzone offerings."

"Lori is amazing, and I trust her completely, which says a lot considering she often has my life in her hands," Shay said. "I can't promise I can reach her, but it's worth a try."

"I say call her," Ryan said. "Then I can tell Sabrina I officially met her and considered her idea of the flight school. Kills two birds with one stone."

Caleb and Bobby eyed each other and came to a silent agreement. "Call her," Caleb said.

Shay nodded and rushed to the phone in the front lobby. Caleb half listened to Bobby and Ryan debate the idea of adding a flight school, but was more interested in trying to make out Shay's conversation.

"She'll do it," Shay said, popping back into the room, "but her brother is in from out of town and took her car out for the night. She needs a ride. I just sent Kent to get her, but he wants to jump with us."

"Of course he does," Caleb said. Now he had a suicidal man, a pilot he didn't know, a gambling addict and Shay—the woman who twisted him like barbed wire—to juggle all at once. Thank God Ryan was coming along because this was going to be one hell of a night.

"I'm going to go meet Mr. Wanted-to-jump-off-a-building myself," Ryan said. "If I might be saving his life tonight, it seems fitting I introduce myself first." He headed to the door, and Shay blocked his exit.

"You aren't going to say anything like that to him, are you?"

"Me?" Ryan asked. "Say something inappropriate? Never." He snorted. "Okay. Not this time."

Shay didn't move, and he added, "I joke around, but I don't play with people's lives."

Shay apparently accepted that answer. She stepped aside to let him pass. Ryan lingered and said, "No wonder Jennifer and Sabrina like you so much."

"What does that mean?" Shay asked. "No wonder they like me so much?"

Ryan laughed. "You'll figure it out."

Bobby sauntered toward Shay. "He meant you don't take any crap, and you know how to hand it out. Two things both Jennifer and Sabrina excel at." He put a hand on Caleb's shoulder. "Later, man. Call me if there are any disasters. Preferably after you've fixed them all."

"Yeah, yeah," Caleb said. "Get the hell out of here and go see your woman."

Bobby laughed, gave Shay a little salute and then headed out, leaving Caleb alone with her.

He cast her a quick inspection. "What happened to changing clothes?"

"I couldn't find the flight suits you were talking about." Hesitantly, she added, "I think I have clothes left at your place. I could run over there and change."

"You don't," he said and walked past her, not sure if he was right or wrong on that point and not caring. She didn't want to be at his place, so she wasn't going to his place. "Let's get you that flight suit."

***

HE WAS ANGRY ABOUT her jumping, and Shay didn't understand why. But she was going to. She was going to right now. Shay stalked after Caleb, not about to let this tension-ridden communication—or, rather, lack of communication—continue.

By the time she caught up with him, he was already in the small storage room, the dim overhead light guiding his search for the flight suits. Shay stood there, studying his profile, and her heart swelled with the feelings she had for this man. Anger faded into something deeper, softer. He'd been there for her today, brave and strong—her hero in so many ways.

"Caleb," she said hoarsely. He turned to face her, so tall and broad, and perfect to her. His eyes were unreadable, his jaw, firm. And Shay forgot what she wanted to say.

He hung a flight suit on the rack near her. "They were shoved way in the back," he said. "No wonder you couldn't find one." He bent down and grabbed a pair of boots, setting them down close to her. He opened another locker and grabbed some socks. "Those are my socks. You won't fit the boots with pantyhose. Don't worry. They're clean." It was a joke but neither of them laughed.

There was a serious note in the air, awareness riddled with tension that Shay desperately wanted to erase. "Thank you for being there for me today."

"That's what family is for," he said softly.

The words hit her like a blast of cold air. "Is that what we are now? Family?"

"I thought that was the point in all of this," he said. "I'm trying to give you what you want."

"All of this," she repeated. "You mean us." It wasn't a question.

"That's right," he said. "Family sticks together, but they don't sleep together. I think that might be a bumper sticker in a few Texas counties."

There was bitterness beneath the words. She heard it, felt it. It was the first time she'd ever heard bitterness from Caleb, and she'd been the one to put it there. She'd hurt him, and that wasn't her intention.

"Caleb," she said, stepping toward him. "I—"

"Shay!" Ryan called. "Oh, Shay. Georgie boy is really needing a you-fix."

Shay wanted to scream at the timing, and because she so desperately needed some connection with Caleb. She pressed her hand to his chest. She could feel his heart race under her touch, and it gave her hope. She lifted her gaze, all but melting in the heat of his stare, and whispered, "I don't want to lose you."

"Shay! Ah, there you are." Ryan had arrived at the storage room, and Shay turned to face him as he added, "Sorry to interrupt you two lovebirds, but George demands your presence. Well, it was more a whimper. Either way, he needs you."

Caleb's hands came down on her shoulders. "Stay here and change. I'll keep him company until you're ready." He maneuvered around her, his body brushing hers. And then, the all-too-familiar feeling of Caleb being gone and of her being left to wonder about the next time, which might never come.

***

LORI DAY HAD ARRIVED just in time for George to finish up his training and was now behind the wheel of their Beechcraft King Air C90G plane. Caleb came aboard and leaned into the cockpit.

Kent was there. "I'm riding up front instead of jumping," he said. "Thinking about taking flying lessons from Lori."

Right. Flight lessons. Funny how he'd never felt that urge until he met Lori. Caleb eyed Lori. "You got a handle on these wings?"

She cast him a scathing look. "If it flies, I can handle it."

"That's what I wanted to hear," he said and left her to check her equipment, thinking Kent was in trouble because the last time he'd seen him as taken with a woman as he was with Lori, she'd been the principal's daughter. And like the principal's daughter, a twelve-year Air Force chick had the power to bust balls. But she was a distraction, and better that Lori bust his balls than a bookie's goons.

Caleb hopped to the ground in front of Shay. George stood off to the side and listened to Ryan tell an Army story as only Ryan could tell it—colorfully. George was actually laughing, while Shay was pale and looked like she wanted to be sick. But still, she was going to jump.

Caleb discreetly pulled her aside. "Tell George you're afraid of heights, Shay." She looked surprised that he knew. "Don't look surprised. Of course, I know. And that's why you're taking flying lessons. You want to take control of your fear."

"How can I urge him to face his fears, to use today as a way to move forward, if I can't do it? Besides, three days ago you wanted me to jump with you. And you weren't happy when I refused." She lowered her voice. "Why, Caleb?"

"Are we ready?" Lori shouted, poking her head out of the plane.

"About time," Ryan replied, slapping George on the back. "George is getting all fidgety on me over here."

Saved by the bell, Caleb thought, because this wasn't the time or place for this conversation. "If you have anything you want to say to George, now would be the time."

She paled. "I can't believe I'm about to do this," she said. "I don't know if I *can* do this."

"Ready, Doc?" George asked, rushing up to her side.

"Are you ready?" Caleb asked George, settling his arm around Shay's waist, trying to calm her. "This is that live-or-die moment we're headed toward."

George nodded in earnest. "I know," he said. "I know."

"We went to a lot of trouble to let you jump tonight, George," Caleb said. "So when you live through this, and you will, then *you live*. No more ledges. You get the urge to jump again, you come here, and you can jump with the Aces. I need that commitment from you." He offered George his hand.

George stared at it a moment, and then shook. "You have it."

"Over here, George," Ryan called.

George eyed Shay. "You okay, Doc?"

She nodded and smiled weakly. "I'm fine." She made a "go" movement with her hand. "See you in the plane."

The minute he was gone, Caleb said, "Not only is there an auto-pull on his chute, but Ryan is both capable and prepared to deal with an in-air complication. He'll be fine." He leaned close, feeling her shake. "Easy, sweetheart. Sure you're up to this?"

She leaned into him. "I'll be with you," she said. "I'll be okay."

His heart squeezed with the words. He wanted her to trust him, but then, she did—with her body. Just not with what he really wanted—her heart.

The next several minutes passed in a fury of engine and wind. Shay stood in front of Caleb, and he strapped them together, molding her body to his. After some stress and nudging from Ryan, George cast Shay a look before giving her the thumbs-up and jumping. Ryan followed.

Caleb whispered to Shay, "Last chance."

She pulled her goggles down in answer. He didn't give her time to think after that. It would only make it worse. He did a final harness check, ensuring she was secured against him, and then jumped. The wind gusted around them, and he could feel Shay stiffen against his body. Within seconds, he'd pulled the chute and had them under cover.

The fall slowed, the view of the Austin downtown lights shining gloriously in front of them. Caleb reached out and pulled her arms to the side, molding them together as one in flight. Letting her know he had her, she was safe. He pointed out a few lights, smiling when she actually responded with an excited wave of her hand.

Too soon, Caleb took them in for a landing in the open field they used for night drops, lights illuminating the ground from fence posts.

And something happened with the feel of ground again beneath his feet. A whirlwind of turbulence unleashed inside him. He cut them free of the canopy, unhooked them and tossed aside his glasses. He turned Shay over and yanked off her glasses.

He framed her body, the hard ground trapping her beneath him. Instant desire burned hot in his limbs, and Caleb forgot Ryan and George were somewhere nearby. His mouth came a breath from hers and lingered, not touching. He wanted to kiss her. He wanted all of her. But she wasn't ready or willing to give him that, and he wasn't sure she ever would be.

That thought brought a splash of cold reality, and he rolled off her and lay on his back, arm over his face. "You jumped for him," he said. "Because you would do anything for your patients. But me—you wouldn't jump for me."

"That's not fair," she said. "I *had* to jump for him. To get him off that ledge."

"I know," he said.

"You know?" she asked. "You keep saying that. What does that even mean?"

He moved his arm and found her leaning on her elbow, staring at him. "It means I know you had to jump for him. Because you'd do anything for your patients."

"You said that already!" She shook her head. "Wait. You mean I won't do anything for you, don't you?"

He jumped to his feet. "I'm not sure. I just want..." he broke off, looked away a moment.

She followed him to her feet, faced him, touched his chest and drew his gaze to hers. "Since when did me jumping out of a plane become the way you judge my dedication to you and to us?"

"It's not about jumping out of a plane, Shay," he said. "And I don't know why that felt so important to me. Actually, I do." Emotion threaded through his words as he continued. "This isn't about the plane and the jump at all. At least, not that kind of jump. I pushed you to jump, to do something that scared you, for me, because I wanted a reason to ignore what my gut told me—that you aren't willing to jump into life with me like I want to jump into life with you. If you were, you wouldn't turn every obstacle into a mountain." George and Ryan were down now, a few feet away. "Your patient needs you." He turned away.

She grabbed his hand and then wrapped her arms around him. Her chin lifted and she stared up at him. Seconds passed and she finally said, "I can't fix this, can I?"

His lips thinned. "I guess not." Because not only was he an all-or-nothing guy, but he was also a realist. If she didn't think she could fix it, she wasn't trying hard enough. Which meant, she didn't really want to.

19

FRIDAY NIGHT, more than a week after talking George off the ledge, Caleb and Kent crowded around the television in the trailer's tiny living room. Kent cursed at a replay of a Texas Rangers game on ESPN when, like Caleb, he wasn't even much of baseball guy. They were both football guys. But they were both looking for a distraction anywhere they could get it—Kent from his upcoming rehab the next day, and Caleb from the silence between him and Shay.

Kent had taken Shay and Lori home that night, and George had gone out drinking with him and Ryan. Go figure. The guy was all right—a bit odd, but wasn't everyone in their own way? And ironically, Caleb had talked to George this week, but not to Shay.

George was coming out Saturday to jump again. He was out of the house and teaching a class on campus instead of from his home as of Monday. At least something good had come out of the day that had apparently been the kiss of death for he and Shay.

Frustrated that he was once again thinking of Shay, Caleb shoved to his feet, walked to the kitchen and tugged open the fridge. And stared. He had no idea what he wanted. Oh, yeah. Shay. Who seemed to think if he was near Kent, he couldn't be near her. He was starting to believe he'd really been her "forbidden fruit" that wasn't so interesting once it wasn't forbidden.

His cell phone rang. He snagged it too quickly, and cursed when he realized he'd actually hoped it was

Shay calling. He grimaced and looked at caller ID. Ryan.

"We're at BJ's," Ryan said, not bothering with a hello. BJ's was the country bar the Aces had started frequenting on Friday nights. "Where are you?"

Caleb opened his mouth to say he wasn't in the mood and shut it again, when he thought of how pathetically he'd reached for his phone, hoping it was Shay. "I'll see you there in half an hour."

"Tell Kent Lori is here," Ryan said and hung up.

That should be interesting. Kent had avoided Lori since the first night he'd met her, and Caleb was pretty sure it was about his rehab. He was embarrassed. Caleb decided he'd leave the part about Lori being at BJ's as a surprise.

Caleb set his phone down on the counter, refusing to be held captive by a phone call that wasn't going to come. "Get up, Kent. We're going out."

"Don't tell me—someone wants to midnight jump and you said yes."

"Nope," Caleb said. "We're going dancing, and I'm getting drunk while you're still around to be my designated driver."

***

AFTER A WEEK OF soul-searching and missing Caleb terribly, Shay was desperate. She knew she loved Caleb and she couldn't bear the idea of losing him. So she went to the place she always went when she needed to truly soul-search. The place she'd been avoiding—she went home, to her mother.

The sweet scent of something yummy baking touched Shay's nose and told her where to find her mother. Sure enough, Sharon White stood behind the kitchen counter, icing a freshly baked cake.

"Hi, Mom," Shay said, trying to sound cheerful when she was aching inside.

Sharon's eyes lit. "Hi, honey. You're just in time to help me finish up my tiramisu. I met this amazing Italian baker on the trip who gave me his secret recipe. I can't wait to see how it turns out. Oh, and guess what? I enrolled in cooking classes down at Central Market. I start next week. I think I might try and open a little bakery someday soon."

"I think that's a wonderful idea," Shay said, so glad her mother had found something she enjoyed. "But actually," she began, swallowing her nerves, "can I talk to you about something?"

Sharon set the knife down and studied Shay more closely. "What's wrong, honey?"

"I just... Can we sit down?"

"Sure, sweetie," she said, wiping her hands on a towel. She headed to the kitchen table and sat at the end, Shay to her left. Sharon touched Shay's hand where it rested on the table. "Oh, dear," she said. "I can see now how upset you are. What's troubling you so fiercely?"

Shay drew a breath and just said it. "I'm in love with Caleb."

Sharon stared at her a moment and then sat back in her chair and chuckled. "You've had a thing for Caleb since you were a teenager."

"No, Mom. I am *in love* with him. Not a teenage crush. Love. I love him."

"I know," Sharon said, as if this were yesterday's news. "Does he?"

"I...well..." She frowned, baffled. "You knew?"

"Of course, I knew. And if I have any inkling of a clue, and I usually do, he's in love with you, too. Is he?"

"He says he is."

"Wonderful," she exclaimed. "So why do you look like someone just took away your dessert?"

"I can't believe you don't see why this is a problem."

"Caleb is a wonderful man, good-hearted. Protective, too. And such a gentleman." She wiggled an eyebrow. "And quite the looker, I might add. Why in the world would this be a problem?"

"If anything were to go wrong between us, I don't want him excluded from the family. He has no one else."

Understanding seeped into her mother's face. "Shay, honey. You don't think much of your family if you believe we would do that to Caleb. We brought him into our family, and he's staying. And people who are family, are family—good, bad and ugly. Finding a person in this lifetime who you really connect with and love is a blessing. Don't let your obsession with 'what if' drive him away." She narrowed her gaze. "Are you sure your hesitation is really about Caleb and the family? Or is there something else?"

"No!" she said, exasperated. "Caleb asked me the same thing. I was worried about him. I told him that."

"And?"

"And nothing. He doesn't believe me. We went from being in love to not speaking. Mom, I'm miserable. I miss him."

"I believe you," she said. "But if you want to fix this, you have to figure out what it is you're fixing. He obviously doesn't feel this is about telling us you two are in love. And something tells me deep down you don't, either, or you wouldn't be here right now. What is it that's really bothering you?"

"Now who's the therapist?" Shay asked, an uncomfortable fluttering in her chest—the truth trying to find a voice. Demanding she admit her fear. Fear.

She'd told Caleb she was scared, but it wasn't about jumping from a plane, and he'd known that. She'd been admitting something deeper, even if she wasn't willing to yet fully face what it was. Nor was it really about telling her parents about her relationship with Caleb. That was there—a part of all of this—but it was really about why she hadn't been ready to tell her parents.

Shay stared at the table, and forced herself to give that fear a voice. "On my eighteenth birthday, I kissed him. The next day—"

"He enlisted," her mother supplied.

Shay looked up, her throat constricted. "Yes. He left. And every time he came home and we connected, he stayed away longer the next time."

"And you're afraid he'll leave again."

She nodded. "Yes." Then stronger, she repeated, "Yes. I didn't want to upset the family, that's true. I wanted to be sure he was here to stay, that we were a sure thing, before I told everyone."

"But you say you love each other," she said. "Why wouldn't he stay?"

"Even though I was pretty certain you'd be happy for us, Caleb certainly was," she said, "part of me can't get over him leaving with barely a goodbye when he enlisted. Or the times he came home and we connected and then he left again. What if we have a fight, and he feels the family is affected? Will he leave again? Will I wake up to find out he's gone, already in some distant country, and I have no idea when I will hear from him again? He says he won't leave again, and I want to believe him. I just...I love him so much. If I let myself really experience what that means, if I count on him, and he leaves again, I don't know if I can bear it. Not this time. Not after all that has happened between us."

Sharon touched her hand. "Tell him that."

"I have. I've told him."

"You told him?" she said. "Just like you told me?"

Shay hesitated. "I feel I've expressed my feelings, but that doesn't change the fact that my gut tells me that he'll leave if things go wrong. I feel it. I know him, and that's the problem. I know I'm right. So of course, I didn't want to tell you guys about us. Why would I shake things up if I feel he could be gone tomorrow?"

Her mother's eyes narrowed keenly. "You just pointed out that Caleb has only us, only our family. He lost his. That kind of thing leaves a mark on a person." Her expression turned thoughtful. "He knows we love him, but I'm sure it's hard to feel he has a real place where he belongs. Maybe, Shay, you sense he's willing to leave because you haven't convinced him you're that place."

Shay squeezed her eyes shut against a sudden pinching sensation. Her mother was right. Shay had been so afraid of being hurt, she hadn't truly given herself to Caleb. If this was their time, as Caleb had said, if she really wanted it to be their time, she was going to have to put herself out there. She was going to have to risk getting hurt.

Shay pushed to her feet. "You're right. You're so right." She hugged her mother. "Thank you so much. I have to go, Mom." She was already walking. She'd been so blind. So worried about being hurt that she'd hurt Caleb. And in the process, she might have lost him.

Shay had her cell phone out and dialed Caleb before she even made it to the car. No answer. She dialed again. Still no answer. "Caleb," she told his voice mail, "please call me. I'm coming over."

Thirty minutes later, she pulled up to the trailer. Caleb's truck was there, but Caleb wasn't. Shay pounded the steering wheel. He wasn't here. Caleb wasn't here. Still, she got out of the car and ran to the door. She knocked. And knocked. No answer.

She started to dial Kent's number but thought better of it. She didn't want to explain herself to Kent right now. Not until she had explained herself to Caleb. She leaned against the door and used her last resource. She called Sabrina.

Sabrina answered on the second ring, the sound of country music in the background.

"Sabrina," Shay said.

"You're looking for Caleb?" she asked.

"Yes," she said. "Yes. I'm looking for Caleb."

"He was as miserable as you, and we talked him into coming out to the country bar we all go to every Friday night." She named the bar and the address, and then added, "He'll be glad to see you, Shay." She hung up.

Shay stood there, shaking inside, but clinging to Sabrina's assurances that Caleb would be glad to see her. Still, she was scared to death of being rejected—and in public made it worse. But she was more afraid of losing Caleb. She couldn't wait. She had to go see him tonight.

***

CALEB STOOD AT A TABLE near the crowded dance floor, not far from the DJ booth, as a Tim McGraw tune wailed from the jukebox about a real bad boy trying to be a real good man. Bobby and Ryan were out there, too, trying to prove they were real good men to their wives. Kent was doing the proving to Lori. It was going to be interesting for sure to see where those two went. Maybe a one-night stand. Maybe more.

Lord only knew, Caleb had tried his share of one-night stands in the early days of the Army, trying to bury himself and the horrors of war and loneliness in a woman. Never worked. Anyone that wasn't Shay had never worked.

Caleb finished off his first beer, the bitter bite adding to his bad mood. He needed another one. He was dead serious about getting drunk. Every heartbroken man deserved one good night of getting legless before they got up the next morning and moved on.

A beer appeared in front of him, brought by a blonde named Heather something—he wasn't sure she'd ever told him—who'd been hitting on him for two months. Every weekend, she'd buy him a beer and he'd turn it down.

"You can take that one," she said, leaning in close so he could hear her. "That's to soothe your broken heart, and don't tell me you don't have one. It's written all over you. So drink the beer. I'm not into being a rebound chick. You're safe."

"If I'm that pathetically obvious," he said, "I'll take the beer." He took a sip. "Thank you."

She leaned on the table. "Who is she?"

"A woman destined for a very long time to break my heart," he said. "I knew, but it didn't matter."

"Because you love her."

"Because I love her."

"Lucky girl," she said. "Maybe I should have a talk with her." She touched his arm. "Hang in there. She'll come around. She'd be a fool not to."

At that moment, Caleb's skin tingled with awareness. His gaze lifted, searched and connected. With Shay's. With the hurt in her eyes at the sight of the other woman next to him. "Shay!" he yelled, but she was already turning and cutting through the crowd. He was not going to get to her.

Caleb's mind raced and he turned to Heather. "Don't go anywhere." He dug in his pocket and rushed to the DJ booth, holding up a big bill. That and the fact that he and the Aces were well known around here would buy him favors. The DJ leaned down, and Caleb made his request.

He grabbed Heather's hand. "Come with me." They rushed through the crowd right about the time the DJ made an announcement.

"Shay White—Caleb Martin requests you wait for him at the door. I repeat, Shay White, meet Caleb Martin at the door."

Caleb was almost to the door, Shay in view, when she grabbed the microphone at the front desk, and made her own announcement. "Caleb Martin, go to hell."

The crowd roared with laughter and cheers, but the announcement had told the doorman, an ex-Army Ranger and friend, Caleb wanted Shay stopped. She was arguing with the guy when Caleb came up behind her.

"Shay," he said.

She whirled and took one look at Heather and turned back around. "Shay, she's not with me." He gave Heather a look of appeal.

"This is her?" Heather asked.

Shay whirled. "Yes, this is her."

"He's telling the truth," Heather said. "He was just telling me about the woman he's in love with, and it wasn't me. It was you. I swear to you there was nothing going on." She glanced at Caleb, and said, "I'm so sorry." And then faded into the crowd.

Caleb walked toward Shay, and she backed away. "Damn it, Shay," he said. "That woman is nothing. But if you need another reason not to be with me, then I guess you can use her. I'm not the problem here. I love you. I'm ready to announce it to the world." He grabbed the microphone on the counter. "I love Shay White." He faced Shay again. "Your brother is here. I don't give a damn anymore."

Frustration overcame him, and he walked to the door and headed outside. He was done. He had no idea why she was here, but it clearly wasn't for the right reason.

"Caleb," she called from behind him.

He kept walking and then realized he didn't even have his truck. Shit. He stopped. The minute he did, she was there, in front of him, hugging him—warm and soft and smelling that special way only she smelled.

"I love you," she said, her cheeks tear-streaked. "I love you so much, Caleb, and I don't care who knows. I told my parents."

His arm wrapped around her waist. "What? When?"

"Tonight. Or my mom, but same thing. I told them tonight, and then I came to find you. They knew, Caleb. Mom said she always knew about us. Caleb, I didn't tell them because I was afraid if something went wrong, you'd leave again. I know you said you won't, but it's hard to put that aside. I'm so afraid of depending on you, and you being gone again."

He kissed her, drank her in with the news that she'd finally accepted them. "Marry me, Shay," he said. "That should be proof enough I'm not going anywhere. Marry me tonight. Let's get on a plane and elope. I've waited for you for ten years. I don't want to wait anymore."

She smiled, tears welling in her eyes. "So if you leave again, I go with you?"

"Shay. Sweetheart." He ran his hand over her hair. "I'm not going anywhere without you. Never again.

Where I go, you go. Starting with an airplane and an elopement destination. I haven't heard a yes. Marry me, Shay."

"Yes," she said. "Yes, a million times over."

"Tonight."

She laughed. "If you can find a place to do it, then yes. Tonight."

EPILOGUE

SHAY STEERED HER CHUTE to the open ground beneath her, hitting the dirt with an easy tumble. On either side of her, Jennifer and Sabrina landed, both laughing as they all cut themselves loose and discarded their goggles.

"That's what they get for telling us we have to wait for them to jump," Sabrina said, eying the second plane overhead.

Jennifer laughed. "And here they come," she said. "They can't stand that we went out alone."

Shay laughed and lay on her back. "I can't believe I did," she said. "Only a month ago I didn't even want to jump." But a month-long honeymoon after an elopement to Italy had included some amazing skydiving scenery, and Shay was hooked on jumping. Caleb was thrilled. She still couldn't believe she was officially Mrs. Caleb Martin and a Hotzone woman.

She and her Hotzone sisters rolled to their backs and watched the Aces, plus one—Kent, no doubt—floating through the sky. Two weeks out of rehab, Kent was determined to make skydiving his new diversion. He wanted to become a jump-master.

"You know," Jennifer said, "Kent and Lori really do sizzle together, but I don't think they've talked since he got out of rehab. Maybe we should arrange something. Besides. I love the idea of opening the flight school."

Sabrina glanced knowingly at Shay. "See what a matchmaker she is? She agrees with me on the flight school because she wants to fix Kent up with Lori. This is why she's a vet—she's very touchy-feely."

Shay laughed. "She did pretty good with you and Ryan."

"She tried to fix me up with Caleb, not Ryan," she said. "That must be a sign that Kent and Lori are completely wrong for each other, because Ryan and Caleb are like night and day, and she had me totally pegged wrong."

"Hey," Jennifer said, leaning up on her elbow. "How do you know it wasn't all my evil plan?" She wiggled a brow. "Make Ryan the forbidden fruit, so you couldn't resist a taste."

Sabrina's eyes lit. "Ryan has a way of making every day feel like forbidden fruit all by himself. He didn't need any help."

Shay smiled because Caleb was on the ground now, walking toward her, mischief in his eyes. Her man. Her husband. And he wasn't forbidden fruit anymore. Though he was certainly good at finding naughty, wonderful ways to show her he loved her. Shay sighed as he tumbled to the ground beside her and onto his back, taking her with him.

He teased her about jumping without him, and they fell into silence, staring at the sky. Shay glanced around, noting the other two couples doing the same thing and contentment settled inside her.

Kent sat alone, staring up at the sky.

Her resolve formed. She was calling Lori.

Caleb laughed and kissed her. "Don't you even think about getting Jennifer's matchmaking bug. He needs to rediscover himself before he has room for someone else in his life."

"I just want him to be happy," she said. "Like I am." She touched his cheek and then glanced at the princess-cut white-diamond ring on her finger before her gaze found his. “I can’t believe we’re married.”

He took her hand and kissed the ring. “My wife. My life.” He smiled and gave her a mischievous wink.

She laughed. “Oh, my husband. My life.”

THE END

Don’t miss the second and third books in the Texas Hotzone series—Jump Start (book one) and High Octane (book two)!

BUY HERE:

https://www.lisareneejones.com/texas-hotzone.html

TURN THE PAGE FOR SNEAK PEEKS INTO TWO OF MY WALKER SECURITY SERIES: THE SAVAGE SERIES AND THE ADRIAN TRILOGY!

EXCERPT FROM WALKER SECURITY: ADRIAN'S TRILOGY

Pri's point-of-view

I exit the bathroom and halt to find him standing in the doorway, his hands on either side of the doorframe. "What are you doing?

"This," he says, and suddenly, his hands are on my waist, and he's walked me back into the bathroom.

Before I know what's happening, he's kicked the door shut, and his fingers are diving into my hair. "Kissing you, because I can't fucking help myself. And because you might not ever let me do it again. That is unless you object?"

That's the part that really gets me. The "unless I object," the way he manages to be all alpha and demanding and still ask. Well, and the part where he can't fucking help himself.

I press to my toes and the minute my mouth meets his, his crashes over mine, his tongue doing a wicked lick that I feel in every part of me. And I don't know what I taste like to him, but he is temptation with a hint of tequila, demand, and desire. His hands slide up my back, fingers splayed between my shoulder blades, his hard body pressed to mine, seducing me in every possible way.

I moan with the feel of him and his lips part from mine, lingering there a moment before he says, "Obviously, someone needs to protect you from me," he says. "Like me." And then to my shock, he releases me and leaves. The bathroom door is open and closed before I know what's happened. And once again, I have no idea if or when I will ever see him again.

FINE OUT MORE ABOUT ADRIAN'S TRILOGY:

https://www.lisareneejones.com/walker-security-adrians-trilogy.html

EXCERPT FROM THE SAVAGE SERIES

I don't just kiss Candace, I ravish her, I drink her in like a man lost in a desert, dying of a thirst he cannot quench. And I was until I found her again. What's worse is, that desert was of my own making, a desolate fucking desert I'm done with because, thank fuck, she's not done with me.

Hugging her close, I hold her like this moment is it, like this is the last time I might ever hold her again. I kiss her just the same, like I will never kiss her again. I've never kissed her with that kind of desperation before now, and not because I didn't love her. I just always took for granted that tomorrow would come. And I always intended to come back, but I didn't and now I know, shit happens. People die, tomorrow is not always guaranteed.

She knows this kiss is different, too. It's in the way she kisses me back, the way she twists her fingers around my T-shirt. In the way she jerks back, parting our lips, searching my face. In the intensity of her green eyes when they meet mine, the sudden parting of lips, now swollen from my kiss, at what she finds, she orders, "Do not kiss me like this is goodbye, Rick Savage, damn you."

She tries to dislodge herself from my grip but I hold onto her. "Don't run."

She gapes. "Run? Me? I'm not the one who ran." I physically flinch with those well-deserved words, but she's not done. "If you want to say goodbye, just say goodbye, Rick."

"I'm not saying goodbye, Candace." I catch her hair around my fingers and drag her gaze to my unguarded gaze. I let her see the torment in me. I let her see the guilt. I let her see the dark need in me that isn't going away like I'm not going away. "This is not goodbye," I repeat. "This is me making sure that you're properly kissed, fucked, licked, and loved, the way you deserve to be."

"It feels like goodbye."

"No, and one day you'll trust me enough to know that a dark night doesn't take us there again. I promise you, you will. Soon."

"How soon?"

"New York. It's going to change everything."

"Can we go now?" she asks hopefully, but we both know we can't. We both know we have to see tomorrow out.

"I wish we could, baby. I wish we could."

My mouth slants over hers, my tongue licking deeply, possessively and I make sure every answer she wants is right there in this kiss. I make sure she knows that I'm not fucking living another day without her. She moans into my mouth and when my hands settle on her spine, she arches into me. I rotate her toward the couch, pressing her against the back, my hands finding that soft smooth skin under her T-shirt.

Goosebumps lift on her skin and I tear my mouth from hers. “You have always been exactly what I need.”

“Am I?”

“Oh yes, baby. You are. I felt you even when you weren’t with me. Every day I was away, I felt you. I missed you. I needed the hell out of you.” I catch the hem of her shirt and toss it, my gaze lowering to her breasts, my fingers tracing the swell above the black lace of her bra, then finding her nipple through that lace.

She sucks in a breath and catches my hand. “Rick, I—”

“God, I love when you say my damn name...”

FIND OUT MORE ABOUT THE SAVAGE SERIES HERE:

https://www.lisareneejones.com/savage-series.html

ALSO BY LISA RENEE JONES

THE INSIDE OUT SERIES
If I Were You
Being Me
Revealing Us
*His Secrets**
Rebecca's Lost Journals
*The Master Undone**
*My Hunger**
No In Between
*My Control**
I Belong to You
*All of Me**

THE SECRET LIFE OF AMY BENSEN
Escaping Reality
Infinite Possibilities
Forsaken
*Unbroken**

CARELESS WHISPERS
Denial
Demand
Surrender

WHITE LIES
Provocative
Shameless

TALL, DARK & DEADLY

Hot Secrets
Dangerous Secrets
Beneath the Secrets

WALKER SECURITY

Deep Under
Pulled Under
Falling Under

LILAH LOVE

Murder Notes
Murder Girl
Love Me Dead
Love Kills
Bloody Vows
Bloody Love (June 2021)

DIRTY RICH

Dirty Rich One Night Stand
Dirty Rich Cinderella Story
Dirty Rich Obsession
Dirty Rich Betrayal
Dirty Rich Cinderella Story: Ever After
Dirty Rich One Night Stand: Two Years Later
Dirty Rich Obsession: All Mine
Dirty Rich Secrets
Dirty Rich Betrayal: Love Me Forever

THE FILTHY TRILOGY

The Bastard
The Princess
The Empire

THE NAKED TRILOGY

One Man

One Woman

Two Together

THE SAVAGE SERIES

Savage Hunger

Savage Burn

Savage Love

Savage Ending (April 2021)

THE BRILLIANCE TRILOGY

A Reckless Note

A Wicked Song

A Sinful Encore

ADRIAN'S TRILOGY

When He's Dirty

When He's Bad

When He's Wild (March 2021)

**eBook only*

ABOUT LISA RENEE JONES

New York Times and *USA Today* bestselling author Lisa Renee Jones writes dark, edgy fiction to include the highly acclaimed *Inside Out* series and the upcoming, crime thriller *The Poet*. Suzanne Todd (producer of Alice in Wonderland and Bad Moms) on the *Inside Out* series: Lisa has created a beautiful, complicated, and sensual world that is filled with intrigue and suspense.

Prior to publishing Lisa owned a multi-state staffing agency that was recognized many times by The Austin Business Journal and also praised by the Dallas Women's Magazine. In 1998 Lisa was listed as the #7 growing women owned business in Entrepreneur Magazine. She lives in Colorado with her husband, a cat that talks too much, and a Golden Retriever who is afraid of trash bags.

CPSIA information can be obtained
at www.ICGtesting.com
Printed in the USA
LVHW091640090321
680887LV00021B/2254